THE PHANTOM BRIDGE

THE PHANTOM BRIDGE

R.T. BYRUM

THE PHANTOM BRIDGE

CONTENTS

CHAPTER I
A Close Call

One of the most frightening ordeals of Dave Carver's life waited for him a few miles ahead, but at this moment his mind was focused on today's trip and on his eagerness for the fun-filled weeks ahead.

It didn't matter how many times he had a chance to fly, Dave always found it an exhilarating experience, and today's flight was no exception. As a matter of fact, he and his younger cousin, Andy Carver, had long dreamed of owning their own plane, or better still, of building one. The wide grin on his face reflected the inner satisfaction brought on by that reachable goal.

"You seem to be really enjoying yourself, my young friend," said the uniformed passenger sitting next to him on the commercial jetliner.

Dave turned away from the window to face the man. "I am," he said. "I was thinking about the plans my cousin and I have for building and flying our own airplane. You can't imagine how great it will feel to finally have our pilot license."

"Oh, I think I can," he said, pointing at the wings on his jacket. "I'm Jeremy Riggs, captain and senior pilot for this airline. Today's the start of a mini-vacation for me, so I'm flying to Denver to spend time with my mom and dad. It's a nice change letting someone else drive."

Dave studied the shiny insignia the captain wore, then realized that he was staring. "Uh—sorry. My name's David Caver, but I go by just plain Dave. I got so caught up in thinking about vacation, I never noticed your wings. Of course, if I had, I probably would have asked you so many questions you would've been glad to see the flight end."

"Very glad to meet you, 'Just Plain Dave'. No need to apologize because I never get tired of flying or of talking about it. Do you live around here?"

"No," said Dave. "I'm visiting Andy, the cousin I mentioned. He lives up in the mountains near Denver with his parents, Uncle Martin and Aunt Karen. His father is my dad's younger brother, and is president and founder of a growing software company."

The pilot nodded. "Sounds like a smart man."

"He is. While still a teenager he earned the money needed to buy his first computer and then began writing basic programs. By the time Uncle Martin got out of college, he had already sold several applications to major companies, and had banked enough money from those sales to started his own business."

Captain Riggs, a good listener, appreciated Dave and his enthusiasm. "So, where are you from and what do your folks do for a living?"

"Captain's Cove on the Gulf Coast of Florida. My dad, John Carver, is lead anchorman on the Channel Seven Nightly News, and mom, she goes by Katie, is an award-winning video tape editor at the same station."

"Interesting. It seems as though you both come from very talented families, Mr. Carver. What's your cousin like?"

"Andy? I guess most people would call him a computer geek...er...whiz. He's following in his dad's footsteps having already written a number of programs on his own. Uncle Martin says he hopes that when retires that Andy will take over the company and market his own ideas."

Dave's seat-mate nodded appreciatively. "Sounds exciting. I hope you two have a great vacation and wish you success in building and flying your own plane. If you'll excuse me, I think I'll go forward and pay my respects to the cockpit crew." Captain Riggs unbuckled his seat belt and squeezed past a flight attendant as she stowed one of the serving carts.

Dave pictured his uncle bragging on Andy's computer skills. He'd been especially animated as he had described Andy's new program that calculated the lift generated by different shaped wings. The cousins were planning to use the program to help design their dream plane.

As their long-awaited project came closer to being realized, Dave found himself becoming even more excited about spending time with Andy. The two had already filled their savings accounts with the reward money earned by assisting in the capture of a gang of armored car thieves on Sea Gate Island last summer, and by helping to recover the stolen vehicle and money. Dave swallowed involuntarily when he remembered how Andy had narrowly escaped with his life when after being kidnapped by the crooks.

Dave turned his attention back to the window. Fields passing beneath the wing were beginning to show the green of new corn, wheat, and soybeans. He loved the Springtime feeling of renewal. From this twenty-five thousand foot viewpoint, he could see the land coming back to life. His eyes moved constantly, trying to take it all in.

The sun's reflection sparkled in the wide river fed by the icy water from melting mountaintop snowfields before rushing along its twisting course to the Gulf of Mexico. He spotted the whitewater rapids where he and Andy often enjoyed wild and wet rides on huge rubber rafts. Towering high above the river were the magnificent Rockies, green at the base, turning to purple where the vegetation thinned. Each was capped by a topping of pure white snow that reminded him of a giant scoop of whipped cream.

A chime sounded. He glanced at the panel above him. The *Fasten Seat Belt* sign had winked on. The First Officer announced preparations to land. Cabin attendants began collecting the drink cups and the leftovers of a simple, but filling lunch. As all the seat backs and belts were carefully checked for proper adjustment, the head steward reminded everyone to remain seated until the aircraft was fully stopped at the gate.

A growling, grinding sound beneath the floor signaled the lowering of the landing flaps. Then came the whoosh of the wheel-well doors opening, and the rumble of the wheel carriages dropping into the air stream. Clank, clunk, clunk. All three landing gears locked, and the airplane began its decent on final approach.

Without warning, the flaps were suddenly reversed and the wheels retracted. Three powerful jet engines roared to full power as the aircraft banked sharply to the left, climbing steeply out of the valley. Carry-on bags, boxes, and briefcases slid from under aisle seats, and coats hung out at strange angles from closets near the restrooms. People screamed, babies cried, and Dave, although trying not to show any outward sign of fear, gripped the arms of his seat, his knuckles turning white with the strain.

Staring out his window, he gasped as a small blue and white twin-engine jet roared out from beneath them with barely a hundred feet of clearance. The jet wash of the huge airliner caused the smaller plane to wobble violently and veer off into a steep dive toward the nearest mountainside. Forgetting his own terror and discomfort, Dave watched in shocked disbelief, fearing that he was about to witness a horrible tragedy.

At the same time, his own airplane was bucking a combination of air turbulence from both the near miss and from the air currents rising from the dangerously close cliffs. Only after the flaps and gear were fully retracted was the captain able to attempt full control of the huge aircraft. Even with his own life in apparent danger, Dave remained riveted to the scene outside his window.

At the last possible moment, the pilot of the private jet wrestled it into a turn, climbing away from near collision with a towering granite wall. Dave's plane was now circling to begin a second approach as the small jet disappeared over the ridge at the south end of the valley. It was as close as Dave could ever remember to being in a crash—an experience he hoped he would never have to face again.

The Captain addressed the passengers over the speakers with an exaggerated western drawl, but with a noticeable quaver in his voice. "Folks, I apologize for the rough ride, folks. We had to hightail it out of the way of a jet jockey who came out of nowhere and ran a red light."

The off-handed manner of their pilot brought nervous chuckles to the shaken passengers and helped to relieve the tension. The attendants moved quickly down the aisle, restoring items that had been scattered about and giving assurance that everything was under control. Again, they retraced the flight path toward the ridge that lay between them and their destination.

As the sleek airliner circled slowly around the highest peak, Dave could see Andy's hometown of Stockbridge spread throughout the valley below and extending well up the slopes of the mountains. His cousin lived in one of these foothills at the edge of town. He spotted the airport, sprawled high atop a plateau. On one side it was bordered by a deep gorge carved out by years of mountain streams as they emptied into the whitewater river flown over moments ago.

Dave watched as his airplane's shadow kept pace on the ground, a dark shape that passed over houses and cars at more than two hundred miles per hour. To one side was the runway, laid out on a table top plateau that towered high above the valley. Passengers and cargo were shuttled to and from Stockbridge by winding road or by one of two cograil trains. The trains, a truly unique mode of transportation, rode up the steep incline from the station at the foot of the plateau to the terminal at the top.

The engine had gears meshed with a toothed rack between the rails so they could make the journey up or down in any kind of weather without slipping. The view during the trip was spectacular, making it an added treat for Dave every time he rode the train.

His attention was suddenly brought back to the present as the wheels touched down in an excellent landing. The thrust reversers on the jet engines channeled the roaring dragon's breath exhaust from the turbines backwards into a braking action. The flaps withdrew back into the wings as the aircraft turned onto the taxiway. Dave began collecting his reading materials—and his thoughts. A slight dip of the nose, and the graceful metal bird finally came to roost at the gate.

It was with a definite sense of relief that everyone unfastened their belts and then began assembling their possessions for deplaning. Each passenger took time to shake hands with and to thank the level-headed pilot who had brought them safely through the terrifying experience.

Captain Riggs was standing outside the cockpit door with the pilot when he spotted Dave. "Captain, this young man was my seatmate until I joined you in the cockpit. Just Plain Dave, meet Howard Mercer, who, in spite of that phony accent he used over the intercom, is really from Brooklyn."

Dave grinned and shook hands. "Captain. Actually, my name is simply Dave in spite of what your friend says. Thanks for a great and exciting ride."

"You're welcome, but I intended to save myself as well as everybody else, so I had plenty of motivation."

"Whatever the reason, there's a whole planeload of people who are glad you were at the wheel. Have a safe trip back, Captain Mercer. And you, too, Captain Riggs." Dave turned and stepped through the door into the jetway.

"Good luck, *Simply* Dave," he heard Captain Riggs call out.

Dave shook his head and smiled as he trudged up the incline into the terminal, his attention turned to the greeting that he knew would be awaiting him in a few moments.

Andy and his parents knew how much Dave loved to ride the incline, so they had parked at the lower station and had ridden the cog-rail up to the airport terminal. Andy was shifting from one foot to the other, occasionally jumping up and down to peer over the crowd at the gate as he tried to be the first to catch sight of his favorite relative.

"There he is!" he shouted so loudly that all eyes turned first to Andy, and then to the arriving passengers. It wasn't hard to see who the young man was looking for. Dave flopped his carry-on bag onto the nearest seat and ran to throw his arms around all three Carvers in one big hug. They were happy to see him, but somewhat startled at the unusually enthusiastic greeting.

Martin recovered Dave's carry-on bag. "Let's get to the baggage carousel before it's mobbed. You can identify your luggage, and I'll load it on the cart we brought."

Karen was full of questions. How is everyone back at Captain's Cove? How are you doing in school? She also made him promise to tell all about the things that had happened during Andy's last visit to Dave's home. The happy chatter continued as they took the shuttle bus to the incline rail.

This time of year the view from the train was especially inspiring. A passenger was able to see most of Stockbridge by looking out first one side of the car and then the other. Andy pointed out the road across the valley that led up to his father's office building. Then he located the intersecting road that rambled past the beautiful home the Carvers had built a number of years ago.

"Wait 'til you see the two ATVs dad bought for us to ride on the trails. We'll be able to explore clear up to the snowline with them," said Andy with obvious glee. The all terrain vehicles had four-wheel drives powered by 350cc engines. Each could carry a passenger and more than two hundred pounds of cargo. They were considered real workhorses in this rugged country.

"Fantastic! I'm really looking forward to spending these weeks with all of you. Dad and mom send their love, and said to thank you for taking me off their hands for a while," said Dave with a chuckle. Then he added in a more sober tone, "After we get to your car I'll tell you about the close call my plane had as we started our first approach. It came close to ending my vacation before it began."

The others grew silent as they saw the serious look on Dave's face. The remainder of the ride down the incline was subdued, with little conversation. The mood continued through the parking lot, into the car, and out the gate to the highway. It was then that Karen Carver turned to face her nephew and asked the question that all wanted answered. "I knew that something was wrong the minute your face lost that famous Carver smile. What happened on the plane, Dave?"

The harrowing details were related to the Carvers, who expressed their gratefulness that someone was watching over Dave and his fellow passengers. In spite of the seriousness of the situation, the relating of the airline pilot's comments brought a chuckle to Karen and Andy.

"What in the world *was* that crazy jet jockey thinking?" fumed Mr. Carver. "He obviously was not obeying the tower's instructions. Our own company plane would never have crossed the path of another in the course of a landing or take off. I wonder where the flight was headed? I'll check into that Monday. We can't afford to permit that kind of irresponsible action to go unchallenged."

"I'm afraid I was too occupied to note his tail number," apologized Dave, "but I'm sure that someone must have seen it. He flew under us, so he must have been planning to cross directly over the ridge instead of making a normal departure turn around Devil's Rock."

Andy, who had been quiet during the telling of events, now added his comments. "You mentioned that he flew out of the valley after the near collision and headed south over the ridge. I'll bet that was his flight plan all along. The local police have had problems with long-range airplanes flying drugs and contraband back and forth across New Mexico to the Mexican border."

"That's true enough, but I'd be surprised if this was a drug runner. I doubt if they'd risk traveling during daylight hours," stated his father. "Nevertheless, we'll get to the bottom of this. Promise you won't let it spoil the rest of your vacation?"

"Promise," said Dave with a nod. He sat back and enjoyed the scenic ride while listening to his younger cousin describe the plans made for their visit together. Near the turnoff to the Carver home was a combination filling station and grocery store where they stopped for milk, bread, and a copy of the local paper.

Andy asked to check out the weather section to see what the forecast for the next few days would bring. "Wow!" he exclaimed. "It's going to be perfect, perfect, perfect! Mild temperatures with bright sunshine. The nights should be clear enough to use my 1200 power telescope and dad's SkyTraker program."

The popular SkyTraker software made it possible to find and identify hundreds of stars and planets. Even more amazing, the program enabled the computer to aim the motorized telescope to the exact position of any object in the sky.

The boys felt that was a great time to be alive, and were pumped up. There was so much to do, that it was hard to know where to begin.

As Andy closed the paper he noticed the headlines. "Oh, no!" he groaned.

Startled by his son's sudden reaction, Martin asked, "What's the 'Oh, no' about?"

"According to this lead story, there's been *another* art robbery, Dad!"

"That has to be the seventh or eighth since they broke into my office," said Mr. Carver through clenched teeth.

Dave sat up. "Wait a minute! Are you saying that somebody robbed you?"

It was Karen who answered. "I should say so. Martin had two very valuable oil paintings and some rare Aztec pottery and statues taken. The insurance settled for the amount we paid for them, but they were irreplaceable."

"What I can't understand is how anyone thinks the stuff can be sold. Most of the robberies have involved art too recognizable to exhibit," chimed in Andy.

"My dad has covered stories like this before," Dave reminded him. "The people who buy stolen art are usually wealthy and are only interested in knowing they own something rare and valuable. They either put it in a private gallery for themselves and friends, or, worse still, they hide the artwork away where no one gets to enjoy it."

"Maybe so," rejoined his cousin, "but sooner or later a piece is bound to be traced to the thieves or to the buyers, and it'll all unravel. That seems like an awfully big chance to take if a thief doesn't plan to sell it."

Since they all knew that there has never been a logical answer to that question, the topic was left up in the air. Still, Dave was already wondering whether or not he and Andy would be able to track down clues to help recover Uncle Martin's valuable artwork. The thought of someone stealing from a member of his family left him with a feeling of anger, of being personally violated.

For now, however, the arrival of the foursome in front of the opening garage doors signaled that it was time to unload, unpack, and unwind. Everyone pitched in to carry Dave's luggage to Andy's spacious upstairs bedroom.

The twin beds had been made up with fresh bedding, and an album of pictures from past visits was lying on the nightstand.

While the two boys busied themselves with putting Dave's clothes in the closet and dresser drawers, Andy's parents went downstairs. Karen was preparing one of her delicious dinners, with freshly baked pumpkin pie for desert. Martin was busy firing up the charcoal grill for steaks and ears of fresh corn.

Mrs. Carvers' cry of despair was followed by the sound of breaking glass. The commotion caught the boys in the midst of storing the empty luggage. They dropped the bags and vaulted for the stairs. Mr. Carver rushed back through the patio doors and met Dave and Andy as they headed for the dining room where Karen had gone to get a meat platter from the china closet. She was standing next to the broken crockery on the floor, but her attention was focused on the wall.

"Oh, not again!" raged Mr. Carver, staring at the empty wall over the sideboard. "This time they've gone too far!" He stormed out of the room to phone the police from the kitchen.

"What's going on?" Dave's confusion shown in his eyes.

"Dad had bought a large bas-relief that had been uncovered during an archaeological dig in the Middle East. It was several thousand years old and extremely fragile.

22

Any mishandling could destroy it. Now it's gone. I doubt if any of our stuff will ever be recovered."

Andy's shoulders shook with rage and Dave felt helpless to offer any comfort. All he knew was that his family had been senselessly violated by crooks without any conscience and his own anger was growing. One thing was becoming clear: spring vacation was going to be anything but dull.

CHAPTER II
Disappearing Headlights

Ten minutes later the police pulled into the driveway at the Carver home. Lieutenant Parker, the detective assigned to the series of art theft cases, arrived nearly an hour later. Martin Carver was fit to be tied, and made sure that Lieutenant Parker knew how he felt.

"First, they broke into my office, and must have known that I also kept valuable artwork in my home. Now even that has been violated by those thieving crooks. You're supposed to be in charge of this investigation, yet you saunter in here an hour after my call. It's no wonder this gang of criminals feels safe to operate in Stockbridge."

Tim Parker was used to insults. They came with the job and had been a part of his life over the past ten years. He understood the frustration of people in turmoil after being victimized. He had learned long ago to handle their complaints with patience. "Most of the victims, including yourself, have been featured in newspaper articles that mentioned your collections. The gang does their homework.

"Let me say I know how you feel, Mr. Carver, but I can't be at two places at once. This is the second art robbery today. I was on the other side of the valley investigating a break-in at the Miller Galleries when your call came in. We're doing all that we can. Apparently a well-organized gang is behind this. The final figures aren't in yet, but the gallery may have lost more than two million dollars in oil paintings, sculptures, and water colors."

Dave could not believe what he was hearing. What was going on? He interrupted the detective with a question. "Why are they picking on your town? Stockbridge isn't that large, and the roads in and out of here are pretty limited. If I were crooked enough to be in their line of work, I'd pick a place that had more to steal." He stopped, and then his face reddened. "Sorry, I didn't mean to offend anyone. I'm sure there's a lot of valuable things that I could find to take."

Andy chuckled. "You always climb all over me for painting myself in a corner. Now it's you that had best stop while you're behind." By this time, everyone was enjoying a good laugh at Dave's embarrassment—everyone, that is, but Lieutenant Parker.

"That's okay, young man. I know what you're trying to say. But Stockbridge is only one of a number of communities around here reporting similar cases. The authorities have all been in communication trying to establish a pattern, and they think that they've found one."

"What type of a pattern are you hoping to find?" Mr. Carver leaned forward anticipating the answer.

"I think it's fair to share some of the information that we've gleaned, but it goes no further than these walls. We have a map full of push pins to mark the locations of the thefts and have kept track of the types of art taken. Several facts are apparent. First, Stockbridge seems to be the hub of these communities. None are more than 200 miles away and they fan out in every direction from here. Second, none of the art taken appears to be contemporary, yet no single piece would be classified as masterpiece. Yes, it's all valuable, and, yes, it's all well-known and prized, but none of it in the class of a Leonardo da Vinci or Rembrandt."

All activity in the room had stopped as each person moved closer to hear about progress in the solving of the mysterious crime wave. The Lieutenant continued. "Many pre-Columbian Mayan and Aztec relics have been stolen." Mr. Carver solemnly nodded his head at the memory of his own missing collection.

"Sir," interrupted a police officer. "We've found something that appears to be another stain similar to the one at the Miller Galleries." He pointed across the dining room at a spot on the carpet near the sideboard.

Lieutenant Parker crossed quickly to the small dark red splotch and knelt with his nose almost against the carpet. "You're right! It's the same and I wouldn't be surprised to find there are more of them at the places we've already investigated. This could definitely be another tie-in between the museum and this residence theft. Send a lab man to backtrack and search for samples. We'll need a few carpet fibers and a swab from each one they find."

Karen, who had kept silent until now, asked, "What do you think those stains could be, and how would they tie in to these horrible crimes?"

"We don't know for sure yet, Mrs. Carver, but I personally believe that it might be a type of hydraulic fluid. If so, the thieves could be holed up somewhere near machinery and might have stepped in a puddle of it. That would explain their tracking it through the places they ransacked today."

"Wow! That could be an important clue if you can pin down the type and manufacturer of that fluid," ventured Dave.

"I wish it were only that easy, son," lamented the detective. "It may turn out to be a common variety. If so, there are hundreds of businesses in the surrounding area that use machinery operated by hydraulics. Every corner garage has car lifts, for instance."

"Still that's a place to start," replied Mr. Carver. "You are welcome to use my computer and software systems to manage any clues that are uncovered. My son, Andy, is quite good at processing data and would be happy to help out."

One of the officers standing nearby moved closer and spoke quietly to Lieutenant Parker. "He's right, sir. Young Carver and his cousin have helped us in bring several other puzzling cases to a close. They've both received awards from the Mayor for their work."

Parker turned slowly and glared at the officer. "You think I've spent these last few years with my head in a bucket? I know all about their amateur exploits and I say, NO! These art thieves are clever, and would be, no doubt, also dangerous if they thought someone was closing in on them. I won't have citizens, especially young ones, getting involved in police business."

"Excuse me, Lieutenant Parker," said Andy in a huff. "Those crooks have broken into my dad's office and into our home. That also makes it our business, no offense meant. You don't have to advertise that any of us are helping. We can do it here at home and modem the results to your office with a password. Only you need to know what we find."

The detective stared out the window. His men were taking plaster casts of tire tracks found near the back door. He chewed on his lower lip as he absentmindedly polished his glasses on his tie. Finally, he turned. "Okay, but I set the rules and you follow them or you're out of it, understand?"

"You've got a deal," exclaimed the cousins in unison. Andy looked at Dave in surprise.

"Come-on!" argued Dave at his cousin's reaction. "I'm just as involved as you are. We're all family. Whatever someone does to you, they do to me. Besides, I'm not going to just sit around on my vacation twiddling my thumbs while you type away. This would be a good time for you to teach me something about computers."

28

Mrs. Carver walked over and put her arm protectively around her nephew's waist. "Dave's right. He has a good head on his shoulders and should be a big help, I would think."

"I appreciate the offer, but I doubt you boys can do much good," said Lieutenant Parker, closing his notebook. "Nevertheless, you deserve the chance to help get back Mr. Carver's art. I'll share what information I can for a start, but you'll have to keep it confidential. Send whatever you find to my attention only. Agreed?"

"Agreed!" said Andy as Dave nodded.

With that arrangement made, the lieutenant and other members of his investigating team began to pack up and filter out to their cars. Minutes later, the Carvers were back in the dining room staring morosely at the bare wall. Martin was the first to speak. "Well, there's nothing we can do right now, so let's get the grill going and have ourselves a fabulous steak dinner."

He didn't expect, nor did he get, any argument.

Even though it was the beginning of spring, the evening air was still quite cool. Nevertheless, the four moved out on the back deck after dinner and enjoyed hot chocolate while they talked about the events of the day. They also recalled the many good times that Andy and Dave had enjoyed together in the past. Then the discussion turned to the packed schedule of activities that Andy had planned for the next week.

It was Mrs. Carver who pointed out a small patch of white near the corner of the house. The Tiki torches that served the dual purpose of providing light and discouraging flying insects threw a soft shimmering glow across the lawn, reflecting off anything shiny or light in color. Andy walked out to see what the unknown object might be. The others saw him stoop, pick something up, turn it in his hands, and then head back to the deck.

"Looks like part of a broken plaster cast of the tire tracks," he announced. "They probably poured a new one and left this one behind."

"You know, that's a tool we should learn to use," declared Dave. "We might even start a collection to help us remember some of our adventures. May I see it?"

Andy placed the cast in Dave's hand. They both moved closer to the torch to more carefully examine the pattern. Several obvious features were apparent. First, the size of the tread revealed the vehicle to have been a van, pickup truck, or a large car. Second, the tire was fairly new, given that the tread was still quite deep and the edges of the pattern were sharp.

The most noticeable thing, however, was the half-moon shaped gouge that ran across one-third of the tread. Like a fingerprint, the mark would make that particular tire stand out among many.

Giving the cast back to Andy to store in a safe place, Dave regained his seat in one of the chaise lounges, then leaned back to drink in the incomparable view of the heavens. He was enjoying the clear mountain air. The cloudless night revealed more stars than Dave ever imagined could be seen with the naked eye. Free from the pollution found at lower elevations, nothing in the atmosphere reflected and diffused the far-away city lights in the valley below. The deep contrast between the pure blackness of the sky and the brilliance of the zillions of stars in millions of galaxies was breathtaking.

Andy suddenly jumped to his feet. "We're wasting valuable time! I told you about dad's SkyTraker program. This would be a perfect night to show you how it works."

Dave was halfway though the sliding doors when he turned to Mr. and Mrs. Carver. "Thanks for the great meal and for letting me spend my vacation here. I can't tell you how much I appreciate it."

"We know you do, dear, and Martin and I are happy to have you here with Andy. We always look forward to your visits," said Mrs. Carver. Like Dave's mother, Katie, she felt that both boys were her sons. There was no more time to express her feelings, however, for the boys could already be heard thundering up the stairs to Andy's room.

While Dave moved the powerful telescope to the large window facing away from the valley, Andy booted up the computer and accessed his software. He motioned for his cousin to join him at the monitor and began to explain how the program worked.

"First we call up this map of the world," he explained, "and use the mouse to point the flashing arrow. . . ."

"The cursor," interrupted Dave.

"Right. Sorry, I didn't mean to get too basic. I forget that you work with your dad's computer, too. Anyway, after you click on the approximate area from where you are viewing the sky, the display changes to a closer view of the globe. Then you click again and narrow your location down even more. You keep clicking and zooming until you pin down the coordinates of where you are as close as possible. Of course, if you already know your longitude and latitude, then you enter them to view exactly how the constellations appeared in whatever section of the sky you've selected."

Dave nodded his understanding. "So you're saying that the screen will show a display that appears the same as if I were looking up the night sky from here?"

"Exactly. For instance, check outside my window and tell me where the brightest star is located."

His cousin glanced in each visible direction, then pointed to a spot about fifteen degrees above the horizon. "There! It looks bright enough to be a planet. What is it?"

Andy checked his computer time and date to make sure it was accurate. He then scrolled the on-screen view of the sky until it showed the northeast quadrant which was the direction that his window faced. A large body was pictured just above the artificial horizon on the monitor. He clicked on it with the mouse.

Triumphantly, he pointed to the text that scrolled across the bottom of the screen. "It's Venus. And here's a summary of what we know about that planet."

Dave was impressed. "I'll bet that would work in reverse order," he said.

"What do you mean by that?"

"Well, what if I entered the local time, date, compass direction, and degrees above the horizon of a known planet or star? Once I matched that section of the sky with the display on the monitor, then wouldn't the longitude and latitude automatically appear to tell me where I was standing at that time?"

"You're right. As a matter of fact, the basic principle of navigating by using a sextant is much like that. The computer makes it a lot easier, and, in most cases, more accurate. We'll have a chance to study lots of stars while you're here. I also copied the program on disk for you to load in your own computer when you get home. Here, it's in this plastic case so it won't get dirty or wet." Dave took the case and slipped it into his inside jacket pocket so he wouldn't forget it.

Andy stood up from his keyboard. "Now, I want to show you how powerful my telescope is. Let's move it to the other side of the room."

After setting it up at the southwest window, Dave aimed down toward the valley and discovered that he could read license plates on cars in downtown Stockbridge—over six miles away! He had tilted the instrument up to watch a night flight take off from the airport when Andy touched his shoulder.

"Look past the runway over toward the mountain. Over to the right—there, near the tower. See those headlights bumping up and down?"

"What about them?" asked Dave, following the erratic vehicle through the viewfinder.

"I don't know of any road over there, and from the crazy gyrations of those lights, the driver must not be trying to find one. Unless I'm badly mistaken, he's headed right toward Killigan's Gorge. That's a straight drop of at least a hundred feet. I hope whoever is driving knows that!"

The boys watched, transfixed, as the bouncing light beams edged closer and closer to the gorge that was hidden in darkness. Suddenly, the vehicle stopped, paused for a few moments, proceeded slowly and smoothly straight ahead ...then disappeared!

"Oh, no!" exclaimed Andy. "They must have gone over the edge."

"I don't think so. If they had, the lights would have dipped down, but they didn't. It's probably some couple parked up there to be alone. I'll bet they'll be coming back in an hour or two."

Andy was worried. "I still think we should report it. At least someone can check it out." So saying, he picked up the phone and made the call. He described the erratic behavior of a car or truck near the gorge and said he was concerned about the welfare of the driver. Asked how he could be so sure of the facts, when he lived on the opposite side of the valley, Andy explained how he had spotted the headlights with his telescope.

The authorities promised to send a helicopter with a spotlight over the area and thanked him for his report. He was also reminded that pointing a high-powered telescope toward the city could make them liable for an invasion of privacy. Properly reprimanded, Andy promised to keep that in mind, then hung up the phone.

"Tomorrow, we can take the ATVs up there and make sure everything's okay," Andy told Dave after describing his conversation with the police.

"Good idea. For right now, I've had enough adventure for two days. Let's turn in and get some sleep."

After the lights went out, Dave lay awake for a long while listening to his younger cousin softly snoring. He started at the sound of a "red-eye" flight taking off, so named because the passengers at that hour were usually bleary-eyed from lack of sleep. In the quiet, the sound of the jet seemed close, and the noise from powerful engines made him relive the moments of terror when his own flight narrowly escaped a deadly collision. Who had been at the controls of that jet? Why was he operating outside the control of the tower? As his eyes began to close at last, Dave seemed to hear the airline pilot say in his shaky drawl, "*That jet jockey came out of nowhere...*"

CHAPTER III
Tracks to Nowhere

The staccato racket of a powerful two-stroke engine jolted Dave out of his deep sleep. He sat up and stared at Andy's bed to discover it was not only empty, but neatly made up. Swinging his feet over the side of his own bed, Dave scooted out from between warm soft blankets, then padded his way to the window. He focused sleepy eyes on the two-story barn that sat more than a hundred yards away at the back of the Carver lawn. Two bright red four-wheeler ATVs sat in front of the double doors. Andy was crouched beside one of them, pumping the throttle while adjusting the carburetor.

Not wanting to miss out on anything, yet always the ideal guest, Dave made up his bed, grabbed his clothes and shoes, and headed for the bathroom. Moments later he emerged—shoelaces flapping, shirttail half-in and half-out, and with his pajamas still draped around his neck, he bumbled down the stairs, tying, tucking, and straightening his clothes. Martin Carver was sitting at the kitchen counter when Dave burst through the door.

"Morning, Dave. I figured you'd be heading this way in a hurry when you heard Andy out there. I told him to let you sleep, but you boys are so afraid of wasting a minute of time together. Incidentally, I got a call from the dispatcher at the police department who gave me a message to pass on to Andy. Said to tell him that they didn't spot anything unusual at the gorge. What was that all about?"

"Nothing that important, Uncle Martin. Andy and I thought we saw a car in trouble at Killigan's gorge and reported it to the police. They must have sent a helicopter to check it out. Guess it was a false alarm."

"You did well to let them know. The police would rather follow up on false lead than take the chance that someone could be in trouble. Oh, one more thing. Are you boys planning to sleep out in the barn tonight?"

"What...? No! Why do you ask?"

"I was wondering what the pajamas around your neck were for, that's all," Andy's father said with a chuckle.

Dave flushed and turned back toward the stairs.

"Thought I'd save you from a worse embarrassment, if you know what I mean. Leave them with me and I'll take them on my way ups to shave. And tell Andy I said to hurry back here to the house so you two can have breakfast before heading out to wherever you're planning to go."

"Yessir," said Dave, handing his pajamas to his uncle. "And thanks for reminding me about these before Andy saw them."

They both laughed, and Dave was out the door.

"Yo, Andy!" Dave waved his arms, then took off at a dead run to the barn.

"Yo back at you! Come on down—the red one's yours," Andy yelled as he pointed at the identically colored ATV next to the one he was adjusting.

"Cute, kid. How would you like one of my famous Dutch rubs on that fancy hairdo of yours?"

Andy's reply was lost as the younger cousin straddled his bike, popped the clutch, and roared toward the house. Seconds later, Dave's four-wheeler sputtered; then added its throaty voice to the racket. He pulled up next to Andy. They switched off the ignitions, waited until their engines wound down and then ran for the deck.

"Hey, we've even got matching helmets. And get this—they're equipped with two-way radios so we can keep in touch. Is this great—or what!"

That called for a high-five on the back deck before they burst inside where Mrs. Carver was already cooking up bacon and eggs. The sweet smell of corn bread wafted from the oven. Breakfast was much like last night's meal in that conversation, between mouthfuls, was a continuation of news, stories, and good-natured ribbing.

"Think there's any chance that we'll hear some news about the robberies, today?" Dave addressed the question to his uncle.

"I rather doubt it. These thefts have been going on for some time. Maybe you boys will get the information on the oil stains, though."

Karen Carver interrupted. "Before you two start rip-roaring up into the mountains, and before you get involved in chopping away at that database, I'll remind you that it's your turn to take care of the breakfast dishes."

Andy sighed. "You mean hacking, not chopping the database, and Dave had already planned to take care of the dishes while I check out the ATVs." He glanced out the corner of his eye to watch his cousin's reaction to being volunteered. Dave's threatening glare was enough to set his aunt and uncle laughing. "Just kidding, ol' buddy," said Andy, feigning fright. "You clear off the table and I'll load the dishwasher."

After the kitchen was in order, Karen helped them to pack their lunches. The morning air was still cool, so the cousins slipped into their windbreaker jackets before collecting the odds and ends needed for adventuring. They assembled a coil of rope, binoculars, a flashlight, camera, compass, snow shoes, a broom, and a map of the mountain trails.

Promising to be home in plenty of time for supper, they scurried out through the patio doors. Andy carefully packed everything on the luggage racks and into the saddle bags strapped to each side of their sleek four-wheelers.

"Let's head up to Killigan's Gorge to check out where the headlights disappeared last night," suggested Andy, mashing his starter button.

Dave tightened the chinstrap on his helmet and nodded. Andy leaned over and showed him how to switch on the radio.

"Hear me, Dave?"

"Loud and clear."

Andy shook his head and pointed to the press-to-talk switch near the clutch. Touching his own switch, he instructed, "Press the button with your thumb when you want to talk."

Dave did as he was told. "Man, that really is loud! How do you turn it down?"

Andy showed him the volume control near the headset jack, then pointed to a path that disappeared into the woods near the barn. "Follow me. I've been through here a dozen times and know all the bumps and turns. Keep it under eighty and we'll be fine."

Try as he might, it was difficult for Dave to keep up with his cousin. This type of vehicle was still unfamiliar to him, although he had owned and ridden a number of motorcycles over the years. It wasn't long, however, before he felt comfortable with the motion and controls of the powerful ATV. Like hares and hounds, they were off and running cross country to the foot of the airport plateau.

"There's a trail that leads up to the back of the airport. If you follow me we can avoid the roads and the traffic."

It took nearly twenty minutes to reach the top of the flattop mountain. Both boys were more than ready to hop off the bikes and rest aching bones and muscles.

"Looks like more fun than it is," groaned Dave, rubbing his tender backside. "The people who make all those great commercials about four-wheelin' either don't do the actual stunt riding or they've become equally numb at both ends."

They laughed and sat on the ground, their backs against a fallen tree, as they watched as one airplane after another launched from the runway a half-mile away. Andy pulled the tab on a cold drink and they took turns drawing long swallows from the can. Dave was tilting back his head for a second gulp when his eyes widened. He gripped Andy's arm.

"That's the jet—Look! I know it's the same Lear jet that nearly crashed into my plane yesterday!"

"How can you be sure?"

"By the make and the color—blue with white trim— and by the wing-tip fuel tanks. Hand me a pair of binoculars," he said, reaching back his hand while keeping his eye on the jet.

Andy ran to his ATV and wrestled with the straps on his pack, but by the time he succeeded in freeing the field glasses, the mysterious plane had disappeared over the south ridge once again. Dave was clearly disappointed, but fished a receipt from his sweater pocket and a ball-point from his camera case. He sketched the pattern of the jet's paint job. Andy watched over his shoulder and nodded approval.

"Maybe someone will recognize the plane from this sketch," Dave said as he folded the paper and stuffed it in his shirt pocket. "Okay, let's head up to the gorge and see about your ghostly headlight beams."

Although no finished road led to the spot where the boys had sighted the mystery vehicle the night before, there was an old horse and buggy trail that wandered parallel to the edge of Killigan's Gorge. Careful not to disturb any tracks, the boys idled their ATVs along the grass bordering the dusty path. There were several shallow ruts, but no clear tread pattern could be defined.

"That's strange," said Andy over his helmet radio. "Whoever was driving had to have come this way. You can see those funny squiggly lines along here, but nothing that resembles tire treads. Might be that the tracks were blurred by rain—or maybe by dragging a bush or carpet behind...."

Dave accelerated away before Andy could finish and stopped near something shiny beside the tracks. Bending down from the seat of his four-wheeler, he picked up the object and was examining it as his cousin pulled alongside.

"What is it?" Andy asked.

"Looks like one of those cheap replacement gas caps. You know, the chrome 'fits all' type for people who leave their old one at the gas pump. It's not rusty or even dirty so I doubt if it's been here long. Wonder if it could've jolted off your vanishing car or truck?"

"I think you're right," replied Andy from the spot where he was kneeling. "Here's a mark in the dirt where the cap first hit, and then rolled over to where you found it. About three nights ago we had a pretty hard rain that would have washed out any traces. That means the gas cap had to have been dropped last night or the night before. The question is...where did its owner go from here?"

Tucking the cap into his jacket pocket, Dave glanced around, then turned back to Andy. "I vote we search the surrounding area on foot and see if we can pick up any clues to the disappearance. We might even find the vehicle itself if the police missed seeing it from the chopper."

Leaving their ATVs and their helmets, they began walking slowly down the road. The sun's angle was low enough to reveal a light coating of new dust on the grass that curved off to the right toward the edge of the gorge. Dave shaded his eyes with his hand as he studied the only path that the vehicle could have taken, given the large rocks and bushes that dotted the landscape.

Realizing that they might have to go some distance, they climbed aboard their ATVs and slowly inched toward the gorge, discovering broken twigs, rocks that had been scattered, and depressions in the softer ground along the way. Eventually, the signs led them directly to the edge. They dismounted and carefully approached the dizzying drop. Lying prone, on their stomachs, they peered over the edge. Eighty feet below a wide stream flowed through the gorge. Old weathered timbers of an ancient bridge stuck out of the water along one side.

"That's been there a long time," observed Dave as he pointed out the brush and debris tangled in the ruined structure. "If someone had driven off the edge, we would see wreckage scattered all over that old bridge down there."

"Maybe so, but there are no marks indicating that anyone turned around and went back. As a matter of fact, it appears that the grass is flattened right to the edge. The guy must have been driving Chitty Chitty Bang Bang and flown off the cliff." Dave nodded thoughtfully at the reference to Ian Fleming's fictitious car that also functioned as a plane or a boat.

Dave collected his binoculars and studied the river-cut chasm that made up the gorge. It was at least forty feet wide at this point. Directly opposite was a granite cliff that rose up yet another eighty feet before leveling off onto a yet higher plateau. Aside from a ledge that protruded a few feet from the sheer wall and several large clumps of bushes, there was nothing to see.

"This makes no sense at all," Dave murmured.

"What doesn't?"

"If that old bridge had fallen straight down from here, it would have to have gone right across to the face of that cliff, wouldn't it? But I don't see anything over there—no tunnel, no road...nothing. Who would have built a bridge to nowhere?"

Andy glanced back down to the hand-hewn timbers below. "It's made out of wood. Maybe it fell upstream and drifted down this way."

Dave shook his head. "It would have been in a lot more pieces if it had smashed its way through all the turns and rapids."

"Not necessarily," argued Andy. "It could've been carried away in a flood a long time ago, then floated downstream in one piece before getting stuck here when the water went down."

Dave conceded that was a possibility. He walked back to replace the field glasses in his pack, then glanced at his watch. "We better put this mystery to rest for right now. If we don't get on with our exploring before it gets much later, we'll run out of time. After all, we did promise to be back for dinner."

Andy unfolded his map. He pointed to a bridge drawn across the same stream. "This bridge is down there in the valley and is the only way across the river, aside from the two highway bridges. To get there we have to retrace our path from the airport, and then head upstream along this trail for about three miles. After crossing the bridge, we'll head southwest to a trail across one of the public grazing lands. That'll take us to the high meadow and the edge of the snow belt."

Helmets in place, radios on, and engines thundering, they spun around and bounced their way back to the dirt road. Behind them across the abyss, concealed amid the artificial leaves of the bushes "growing" on the ledge, a tiny video camera turned on silent gears, following their retreat from Killigan's gorge.

CHAPTER IV
The Old Abandoned Church

By the time they had left the valley bridge and had reached the high meadow, the noonday sun was directly overhead. Lunchtime! Parking their four-wheelers where they could look down over the valley, the cousins eagerly unwrapped sandwiches and pulled the tabs on their drinks. The adventure their ride and discoveries, and the crispness of early spring in the mountains had sharpened their appetites.

The slope of the meadow rising behind them led ever higher until a scattering of snow mixed with the emerging green of new plant life. It was as if a line dividing spring from winter had been drawn across the face of the slope. Everything above the line was painted with the pure white of snow that would hang on for weeks before surrendering to the warming of a triumphant sun.

As they ate, Andy located some of the landmarks they could see from their vantage point. He proudly pointed out his own home, which lay across the valley directly opposite their impromptu picnic spot. Below them the airport plateau was split into two parts by Killigan's gorge—the nearer section higher than the runway. Perhaps a million years ago the whole valley had been under water and level, but the ancient river had gradually receded, slicing away at different levels of soil which it carried southward toward the Gulf. The erosion also left mesas or flat-topped hills scattered throughout the mountain range.

"Who was this Killigan?" asked Dave, his words filtered through a mouthful of potato chips.

Andy, engrossed in his corned beef and Swiss cheese sandwich, was caught unawares by the sudden question. "Who?"

"Killigan—you know—the guy the gorge was named after?"

"Oh, him. He was supposed to have been a miner who made a big gold strike in these mountains. The story goes that it was his gold that brought people here to settle what was to become the town of Stockbridge. They say his mine is somewhere here in the gorge...but it's never been found. Maybe the 'Carver Private Investigators' will discover it! How's that sound to you? 'Carver P.I.'s—*Mysteries Solved While You Wait.*' Cool, huh?"

Dave lowered his binoculars and turned to stare at his cousin. "The thin air is really getting to you, Andy." He swung back around and returned to sweeping the landscape spread before him. As his gazed traveled down the length of the gorge, he suddenly backtracked and adjusted his focus. "What's that?" he asked, pointing to a white-steepled building atop a higher plateau.

"Only an old church abandoned years ago. Shepherds who used to live up in these meadows built it in the 1800's.

Actually, Stockbridge was named after the bridge used for herding the sheep across the gorge to the grazing meadows behind the church. After the valley became industrialized, the sheep business more or less dried up. No one these days wants come all the way up here to attend a church that's practically next to an airport runway."

"Then why is someone filling the heating oil tank?"

Andy took the field glasses from Dave and zeroed in on the church. "That *is* strange," he agreed. "Guess the building's being used after all. Bet it would be interesting to see the inside, being that it's so historic and all. Think anyone would mind if we peeked in?"

"Probably not, but if we're going to carry out our other plans, we'd better put the visit off until another day." With that, they began clearing up the few leftovers from their lunch, and stowed them along with the wrappers and pop cans.

They decided since their picnic coolers were now empty they would go up to the snow line and pack them full of snow to take back home. Stored in plastic bags in the freezer chest until later, the snow would be used for a sneaky ambush. The mental picture of the look on their friends faces after being pelted with snowballs on a warm spring day was enough to set them off into fits of laughter.

Twenty minutes later, the Carvers were plowing through foot-deep powdery snow. They stopped long enough to add sweaters beneath their jackets and to don their gloves. The rugged ATVs charged effortlessly forward and upward until the boys found wetter snow that was the right consistency to form smooth round missiles. Both coolers were topped off with ammunition, and then it was time to head for home. But first, there was one more part of their day's plan to be fulfilled. Moving still higher to reach a clean white slate of snow, they lined up their ATVs in single file and carefully drove in a pattern to write one giant word in the snow...*CARVER.*

Parking his vehicle a short distance away, Andy donned his snow shoes, and, with the aid of the broom, smoothed away the tracks around and between the letters.

The cousins returned to the lower meadow and spun around to view their handiwork. The writing was big enough to be seen clear across the valley. Andy's mom and dad would really be surprised when they pointed it out to them. The approaching sunset would create a drop shadow on the letters and make them even more pronounced.

Dave nodded his satisfaction at their "penmanship," and, pointing his mount toward the return path, popped wheelie before roaring downward through the meadow. His cousin met the challenge by shifting quickly though his gears to match Dave's pace and was soon alongside.

Andy's voice came over Dave's helmet headset. "Think we should show that gas cap you found to the police? They probably thought we were crazy sending them up there to check last night."

49

Dave keyed his own radio. "What's the use? There's no way to prove how long it had been there. I think we'll hang on to the cap, and see if we can find out who lost it."

His younger cousin burst in. "You know what? I just remembered something about that church."

"What?"

"Well, it wasn't exactly about the church. It was about the oil truck"

Dave began to slow down. "What about the oil truck?"

"Actually, it *wasn't* an oil truck," Andy rambled on, much to Dave's frustration. "I mean it seemed like the kind that carries heating oil, but I now recall that the sign on the tank read *Gasoline.*"

Dave stopped and so did Andy. "Are you sure?" asked the older Carver. "They wouldn't deliver heating oil *and* gasoline in the same truck. I don't even think they use the same type of nozzles. And, why deliver gasoline to a church in the first place? This doesn't make sense."

"Maybe it's for a lawn mower? Nope. They wouldn't bring up a whole truckload for that. Well, that's something we'll have to investigate. Let's see, we have about ninety minutes before we promised to be back for supper. That should give us enough time to swing by." He smiled and spun his handlebars toward the steeple in the distance.

Up close, the clapboard church appeared abandoned and weather-beaten. Many of the stained-glass windows were cracked or broken. Standing on the luggage rack of his ATV, Andy peered into the sanctuary through a window that was missing most of its biblical scenery. Most of the pews were either shattered in pieces or leaning drunkenly on splintered supports. Evidence of senseless vandalism was everywhere. Except for a few scattered footprints in the thick layer of dust on the floor, there were no signs of habitation. Why, then, would a fuel truck be delivering gasoline to this abandoned building?

"Listen," urged Dave. "Do you hear that sound?"

Both strained to discern the low murmuring rumble above the constant bluster of wind across the mesa. The source seemed to be from the back of the church. The level increased as they approached the rear of the building. A steeple rose high above them, and air around the belfry seeming to ripple with heat waves flowing out of the bell chamber louvers.

"That's odd," observed Dave. "As cold as it is up here, why would we see evidence of heat coming from an empty building?"

Andy placed his ear against the weathered sideboards. "Maybe it's not heat. Sounds like a large engine is running inside the church. What's going on?"

"I don't know, but let's try the front door to see if it's locked. We should be able to solve this mystery in a few minutes."

The door was not only locked, but posted with a "NO TRESPASSING" sign. It was hand-lettered and obviously not an official notice.

"I know for a fact that the original owners are no longer around," stated Andy. "Whoever put up that sign must be using this building for another purpose. Think we should try to get in through one of the windows?"

Dave shook his head. "There's no reason to get ourselves in trouble with the law. We can check with the Stockbridge police to find out who officially owns it. If it turns out that no one has a current claim on it, we can always come back. I'm just as curious as you..."

Blam! Blam!

He was interrupted by two sharp reports accompanied by heavy thuds as slugs slammed into the wooden wall right over their heads. The boys ducked and ran for their four-wheelers. Crouching low behind them, they pushed the ATVs around the corner of the church and found shelter behind a tool shed.

"Someone shot at us!" cried Andy, his eyes wide with amazement. "Real bullets! They were trying to kill us!"

"Maybe not. It could have been a couple wild shots from a hunter."

"Do you believe that?"

"No...but I'd like to. It's also possible that we're sticking our noses into a place where we're not welcome. Let's keep the church between us and whoever fired those shots. We'll make a zigzag run far enough away to get out of range, and then circle back to the trail down the mountain."

Keeping low over their ATVs, Dave and Andy wasted no time putting distance between them and the mysterious trigger-happy gunman.

The sun was beginning to disappear behind the peaks as the boys pulled into the driveway of the Carver home. They idled into the barn and shut down their engines. The boys were silent as they removed their helmets and gloves. They had started for the house when Andy touched Dave on the arm. "Dave, let's keep this to ourselves for right now, okay?"

Hesitating at first, but then with a nod of assent, Dave put his arm around Andy's shoulder and they headed in for supper. Karen Carver was putting the final touches on the table setting as the boys closed the doors to the back deck.

"Well, how did the day go for our mighty explorers?" she asked with a smile.

"Great!" was the reply in unison, but they couldn't help glancing at each other with a touch of guilt in their eyes. Should they tell about the shots fired at them? Until they knew for sure whether or not it was an accident, they would stick with their decision to learn more before saying anything.

"Where's dad?"

"He'll be down in a minute, Andy. You fellows wash up. Supper will be ready in about five minutes."

The cousins returned to the kitchen in time to see Martin enter from the library.

"Dad...Mom. Come here to the window," urged Andy. "We've got something to show you."

Andy handed each of them binoculars and pointed to the snowline that proclaimed the Carver name in huge letters. The setting rays of the sun deepened the ruts and the letters stood out clearly against the white background.

Andy's parents smiled broadly at the artistic imagination of the lively teens.

"Now that's a clever idea! Maybe I should hire you boys to advertise my company," said Martin. "Everyone in the valley will be able to read that for several days. That goes double for people flying in and out of the airport. I could save a bundle on my billboard budget."

"Not necessarily so," replied Andy. "You don't know our fees. But you're right about one thing. A lot of people will know the Carver name when the sun comes up in the morning."

Unknown to the Carvers, the name had already been seen on the mountain by those interested enough to search out their address. One of them was sitting at a table in a chamber far beneath the old church, carefully cleaning his rifle before replacing two recently fired shells.

CHAPTER V
Another Robbery!

Martin Carver was furious when he called from the office.
His wife had never known him to be so upset. He had met
Lieutenant Parker in the company garage, and the news the
detective had brought him was not good.

"The police found our stolen bas-relief lying in the
service road behind the Stockbridge Museum—smashed
into small pieces. The investigators can't tell if the thieves
accidentally dropped it or if it was deliberately destroyed. I
have to go to the crime scene to identify the pieces."

"I'm so sorry, Darling. I'm also concerned about what
our insurance company will think about these robberies—
first your office and now our home. They may suspect that
we had something to do with this."

There was a silence on the line, and then her husband
spoke quietly. "Are you suggesting that our recent contract
loss with the government might cause them to believe we
staged these robberies for the insurance payments?"

"I'm not trying to upset you more, Martin, but I think
we need to be aware that it might appear to be suspicious."

Martin's tone was softer. "Don't worry, Karen. In the
first place, we are only one of a number of victims. In the

second place, we have new contracts about to close that more than make up for our losses. Okay?"

"Yes. You're right, of course. Who can be responsible for these horrible crimes?"

"I don't know, but I intend to find out. Lieutenant Parker brought me a stack of records for the boys to run through the computer. He seems genuinely interested in solving this crime wave and eager for any help he can get. I'll be home after I identify our artwork."

Karen hung up the phone and sank into a kitchen chair to finish her rapidly cooling cup of coffee. She was still there when Dave and Andy came down for breakfast.

"Why the long face, Mom?"

Andy's mother recounted the story as she prepared their breakfast. Seeing his mom so upset, and knowing what the robberies were doing to his father, made the young man both sad and angry.

"Dave...we've *got* to do something. These guys can't be allowed to get away with this. Everyone for miles around will be afraid to leave their homes unattended for fear they'll be the next target."

His cousin finished chewing a large bite of bagel and cream cheese. He washed it down with hot chocolate before attempting to speak. "Sorry. You caught me with my mouth full. We *have* a chance to do something. As soon as Uncle Martin brings those records home. There has to be a pattern. We'll find it once we finish processing the data in your computer. Your dad said Lieutenant Parker is sending us their findings on the hydraulic fluid stains, as well as the robbery locations, and lists of what was stolen at each crime scene."

"I'll prepare a spreadsheet template on my computer," declared Andy. "That'll be the fastest way for us to begin organizing the data." He pushed away from his half-eaten breakfast and was immediately surprised to feel himself sliding back under the table again. He glanced back over his shoulder to see his mother remove her hands from the back of the chair and place them on her hips.

"Not so fast, my young geniuses. We'll discuss what you can and cannot do about working on this case while you're finishing the breakfast I made for you. I know how it is with you two. You always start by merely 'processing information' and the next thing I know, you're out trying to do the work of the police department. The money involved tells me that this gang of thieves wouldn't hesitate to attack anyone foolish enough to mess with them."

"Aunt Karen, Andy and I know better than to tangle with them," Dave assured her, "but the crooks have picked on our family. We can't stand by and let that happen. Who knows? It's possible that the Carver Private Investigation Agency will come up with the clues to break the case."

"*The Carver Private Investigation Agency?*" Karen made a wry face.

Dave shrugged. "Ask your son."

Andy jumped in before his mother could pursue the question. "Sooo—when did dad say he'd be home with the records?"

"He told me he'd be home right after identifying our bas-relief—probably around lunch time," she answered, glancing at her watch. "What are you planning to do until then?"

Andy glanced at his own watch. "We have time to run down to the museum and then meet back here with dad. I'd like to know if they've discovered anything more about how dad's artwork ended up in the street there. We can't legally drive the ATVs through town, though. Is it alright if Dave and I take the station wagon? He's a careful driver, and has his own car back home, you know."

Karen Carver knew of her nephew's spotless driving record, and of the street-legal dune buggy that Dave and Andy had built over the past several years. Indeed, thanks to her son's enthusiastic description, she felt as though she had personally ridden in the *SandWitch*.

"Yes, of course. But I will expect the two of you to be back before your father gets home. He wants to go over the records with you before he returns to the office."

"We promise," said Dave, accepting the wagon's keys from his aunt. "If there's anything that you need from the grocery, we can pick that up, too. Andy wants to buy a new package of floppy disks at the computer store next to the Winn-Dixie."

"As a matter of fact, I do have a short list of things we need for dinner and for tomorrow's breakfast. I'll give you some money, and you can pick up the list from the hall table on your way out. Thanks for saving me the trip. You boys be careful. Okay?"

With a nod, they were off to the garage. Minutes later, the family station wagon was headed for Stockbridge. The day was beautiful. The cousins almost regretted that they had decided to work indoors on the police records. Still, the vision of Andy's powerful computer chewing up the raw data and spitting out valuable clues made it worthwhile.

Andy's voice cut into Dave's thoughts. "We'll use my mapping software to mark the locations of all the reported robberies within several miles. Once we print it out, we should be able to see if there's a pattern that shows up around Stockbridge, as the lieutenant suggested the other day. If the crimes *are* all related, and the thieves fan out from a central point, then we might be able to spot their hideout on the map."

Dave grinned at the excitement in Andy's voice. "Right. And we can also check the lab results on the hydraulic fluid stain against the formulas Lieutenant Parker said he requested from the various manufacturers. If we can narrow down the type, even the brand, it may give us a clue as to the kind of machinery the crooks were around when they stepped in it. We don't need to do everything in one day, though. Let's spend time outdoors, and work on the clues this evening."

Andy agreed, then pointed out the top of the museum that poked above a low shopping center several blocks ahead. Dave wheeled the big wagon through the streets until a patrolman standing next to a road blocked with crime scene tape stopped him.

"Sorry, boys," the policeman apologized as he leaned down to peer into the wagon's open window. "Museum's closed. We've had a break-in and the lab boys are busy collecting evidence. You'll have to detour around by going two blocks down 14th, and then turn left on Briel Parkway. That'll bring you right back on this road about a half mile further."

Dave listened politely and then asked, "Is Detective Lieutenant Parker in charge here?"

The officer was surprised at the question. "Yes, he is. Do you know him?"

"He's working on my uncle's robbery. His office and home were both broken in to. This is Andy Carver, his son, and he and I have come to see the smashed bas-relief that was stolen from his home. I'm sure the lieutenant will let us do that."

After a thoughtful pause, the policeman triggered the radio mike pinned to his uniform. "Unit 34 to Lieutenant Parker."

A voice came back immediately. "Parker, here. What do you need, 34?"

"There's a station wagon with two young men named Carver with me, who claim to know you. They'd like to view the broken artwork that they say was stolen from their home."

"Mr. Carver has already been here, and is headed to my office to pick up some papers. He's already identified the sculpture, but it's okay for the boys to have a look, too. Let them through, but have them park their wagon outside the scene. We're working on tire tracks in here that we don't want disturbed. I'll send an escort for them to your post. Parker out."

Dave moved the wagon to the spot pointed out by the officer. They returned to the barrier at the same time that their escort arrived. "Are you the Carvers?" the man in the blue overcoat asked.

"Yes, sir," answered Andy.

"This way."

The side lawn and service road were literally crawling with technicians who were on their hands and knees, collecting everything from tire casts and footprints to close-up pictures of the shattered art. The boys were fascinated with the quiet efficiency of the scene. Each person was so fully engrossed in his or her task the two cousins were basically ignored.

Andy tugged on Dave's sleeve. They both came to a halt when Andy pointed to a patch of mud in the gutter. Their escort continued ahead, oblivious to the temporary loss of his charges. They moved closer, and then squatted next to tire tracks that ran through the still moist dirt. Clearly imprinted in the pattern was the same half-moon gouge that they had seen on the broken plaster cast the police had left behind at the Carver home.

The man in the blue overcoat turned to see the boys fifty feet behind him. He quickly strode back to them with a warning. "Don't touch a thing! Move away from there and stay with me. Everything is a potential clue, and the Lieutenant would have my head if you messed up his investigation."

"We're sorry," offered Dave. "We understand that it's important not to interfere, and would never have touched anything. It was that tire track. It seems identical to the one at our house the day of the robbery."

"That's what we've concluded, too," said the man in a calmer voice. "Lieutenant Parker had already ordered a cast made and compared it with photos of the one at your place. But even without that clue, it's quite evident that the same gang is responsible for most of these robberies."

Andy studied the man's face. "You mean because the bas-relief taken from our house was found broken in the driveway here?"

"That, and other things," volunteered their escort.

"Like hydraulic fluid stains from someone's shoes," asked Dave.

The man's manner changed abruptly. "I didn't say that! We're busy, so if you want to see the Lieutenant, let's go."

Andy and Dave exchanged knowing looks as they approached a harried Detective Parker.

"Hello, boys," came the greeting. "There's your smashed artwork, but don't cross the tape or touch anything. I'll be with you in a minute."

It was a disturbing sight. The irreplaceable relic had been destroyed in the blink of an eye by ruthless criminals after having survived centuries of man and nature. Who *were* these people? Where were they hiding? How were they unloading the stolen goods? Why were they picking on Stockbridge? What was the source of the stains from their shoes? So many questions, so few answers.

Lieutenant Parker returned, studying a pad filled with notes. He glanced up at the boys as he approached. "Well, the tally really climbed today. This gang made off with paintings by Rossetti, Goya, and a first edition Emerson manuscript. The totals aren't in yet, but added to the rest of the take, the loss will be over three million dollars."

Andy gave a low whistle at the huge sum of money.

"Including the Miller Galleries job and the artwork from your dad's home and his office, I'd say they've hit Stockbridge for more than six or seven million dollars in three days. The Mayor'll have my head and my badge for sure." Realizing that he had probably said too much in front of the young men, he reddened, and began flipping rapidly through the pages of his notebook.

"Lieutenant," said Dave in a soft voice. "We're sorry this is happening, and we want to help. When Uncle Martin gets us the records, we'll start on them right away. We promise you'll hear from us the minute we learn anything."

He extended his hand, and the detective grasped it firmly. The barest suggestion of a smile eased the hard lines on Parker's tired face.

"Thanks. Even if you come up with nothing, I appreciate your concern. Now I'd suggest you head back home and meet Mr. Carver. I know he's expecting to brief you from the notes I furnished him earlier. If we turn up anything to add to the data bank, I'll be in touch with you. You know the way back, so you won't need Charlie to escort you. Just watch where you're walking." He turned and headed toward the entrance to the museum as the cousins retraced their steps to the car.

"Seven million dollars!" exclaimed Andy as Dave pulled away from the curb. "These aren't your ordinary everyday crooks. These are big league players. I can hardly wait to see what my computer thinks of the meal we're about to feed it."

Dave accelerated up the ramp, then onto the four lane highway leading toward the Carver home. "That's one of the things that bothers me. If these guys are serious enough to steal millions, then wouldn't they also be serious enough to shoot at anyone that comes close to their hideout."

Andy's eyes were wide as he turned to Dave. "Are you suggesting that the bullets fired at us up at the church could be related to these robberies?"

"It's a long shot, if you'll pardon the pun, but I think we should scope out more of the roads and trails around there for tire tracks with a half-moon bite out of them. That includes the area around Killigan's gorge where we found the gas cap. Why would anybody go to the trouble of wiping out their tracks up there unless they didn't want to be followed?"

"Still, we're putting together nothing more than a bunch of circumstantial evidence in trying to tie all those things—the old not-so-abandoned church, headlights at the gorge, the robberies.... Unless we find the missing artwork, the source of the hydraulic oil stains or the half-moon tires, we're as clueless as poor Detective Parker."

Dave drove in silence for several more blocks. "We may know more than we think I don't believe for a second that those shots fired at us this morning were an accident. No...someone wants to scare us away from nosing around the church."

"As far as I'm concerned," said Andy, "they've done a pretty good job."

"You mean of keeping us from nosing around?"

Andy chuckled. "Not in a million years. I just meant they did a good job of scaring us, but it will take more than a few well-placed, close shots of a large gauge rifle to keep Andy Carver, Private Eye, away."

Dave glanced at his grinning cousin, shook his head, and turned back to the road. Spotting a Winn-Dixie grocery, Dave remembered his promise to pick up food for his aunt. He expertly steered the wagon into the mini-mall and found a parking place in front of the office supply store where Andy could get his pre-formatted discs. While the younger

Carver disappeared inside, Dave hurried to the grocery to pick up the items on his aunt's list.

A few minutes later, the two emerged from the different stores and met at the station wagon. The small car parked to the left of them was gone. In its place was a dark green extended-body van with tinted side windows. Dave had to squeeze through the narrow space between the two vehicles then carefully wriggle his way into the driver's seat. As he fastened his seatbelt, Andy heard him muttering under his breath about inconsiderate drivers.

Laughing at his companion's grumbling, Andy managed to keep an eye on the narrow gap between them and the adjacent cars as Dave began backing out. "Stop!" he cried. Dave slammed on the brakes, pinning Andy and the groceries against the seats.

"What?! I wasn't about to hit anything!"

"I know that," said Andy. "Look at his gas cap."

Dave craned his neck around to see the rear of the van. "What do you mean? There isn't any…" He reached into his jacket pocket and pulled out the cap they had found near the gorge. "Are you suggesting this van is the vehicle we saw the other night at the Gorge simply because might be the one that lost this cap? The problem with your theory is that dozens of cars have a cap missing on any given day. We need something more concrete than this for a clue," he stated as he tucked the object back into his pocket.

Andy fished the grocery receipt from the sack and scribbled the van's license plate number on the back of it.

"Just in case," he said, putting the paper in his pocket and returning the ball point pen to the visor pocket.

Dave finished backing out, shifted into forward, and carefully made his way through the narrow aisles of the parking lot. Unnoticed by either of the boys was a puddle of water twenty feet behind the green van. The vehicle's wet tire tracks emerging from one side of it showed the distinct pattern of a half-moon repeated several times.

The rest of the trip home was made in silence. The cousins considered the implications of their discoveries. What if the gas cap they found was the one from that van? What if their suspicions were right, and the church turned out to be the key to solving the crimes? What if those two shots had been only a warning, and any future ones were for real? While it was too early to jump to conclusions, they would be much more cautious in their snooping around.

The boys turned into the driveway and parked behind Martin's sedan. At the same moment, in the dusty office of the old church far across the valley, a bearded figure in oil-stained clothes dropped an open phone directory on the scarred top of an ancient desk. The man in the chair behind the desk pulled the book closer without so much as a word or glance to acknowledge the other's presence. A name and address was highlighted in transparent yellow in the middle of the page.

"Are you sure this is the right one?" he finally asked, loosening the clerical collar on his shirt.

"Yep. One of the kids on the four-wheelers is his son. The other's his nephew. They was the ones writin' the old man's name in the snow. Nice of them to leave a calling card." The bearded one snickered noisily.

A harsh glare from the other silenced and sobered him. "If they come back, get rid of them and their bikes, but not around here. Dump the four-wheelers far up the gorge where the water's deep enough, and take the boys out on the next trip over the Gulf. I want them anchored down with enough weights that they'll *never* be found."

CHAPTER VI
A Pattern Emerges

It was the boy's turn to do up the dinner dishes. Andy was using the sink spray to rinse off the loose food before loading the dishwasher. Dave brought over another stack from the table and watched his cousin with the sprayer.

"I was thinking about the strange...what did you call them? Oh, yeah. The strange *squiggly* marks on the road next to the gorge," Dave said, picking up one of the spray-rinsed dishes. He held it up side by side with one of the soiled plates. "If it *had* rained up there, the tracks would have been washed off—just like your sprayer flushed the traces of food from the plate."

"Yeah, but it didn't rain that night," interjected Andy.

"Exactly my point. But you mentioned one way to get rid of tracks. Back in the Old West, Indians used to drag sagebrush behind their horses to wipe away their hoof prints." Dave lightly wiped across the soiled plate leaving a blurry mixture that bore no resemblance to the original pattern of leftovers. "What if our mystery car or truck *did* have a bush or a rug or something pulled behind it?"

"I wasn't being serious, Dave. Even if that were the answer, why would anyone go to all that trouble to conceal their having been there? I bet it was only teenagers parking up at the gorge, and they wouldn't go through such elaborate pains to cover their tracks. Besides, there's one other thing we're overlooking."

"What's that?"

Andy returned the sprayer to its socket, then turned to face Dave. "You and I watched the gorge for a long time. The chopper was up there, too. No one but the two of us saw the headlights going there, and no one saw them leave. So—where did they go?"

Dave turned this angle over in his mind then shrugged. "Who knows? Let's hurry up with the dishes so we can begin processing the data your dad brought home. I promised Lt. Parker that we would have answers for him as quickly as possible. We can start by seeing if the center point of these robberies point to the old church or the area around it. I have a nagging suspicion that all of this ties neatly together."

It was long after dark before all the robbery coordinates had been entered into the mapping program, but at last the results were ready to be printed. Andy and Dave watched in fascination as the map, centered on Stockbridge, emerged from the laser jet printer. Andy took the original and ran it through the copier, then laid the copy on the desk in front of Dave. "We'll mark this one up and keep the original in case we need more working copies."

Dave agreed, first circling the general area of Killigan's Gorge and the church with a highlighter pen.

Using a straight edge, he connected all the robbery locations to the circle. He stood up to study his handiwork.

"See? The farthest locations in any direction are less than four hours from Stockbridge, and most of the thefts are within two hours. Notice that there's no other town on this map with so great a concentration of crime scenes as we have in your town. That's why I'm sure that their hideout must be around here. My vote is that it's connected to the church."

Andy tapped a pencil on his front teeth and nodded. "I think it's worth checking out. Should we fax this to the Lieutenant tonight?"

His older cousin wrestled with the question, and then shook his head. "The police already have a record of our report about the disappearing headlights in that general area. Unless we can back up our theory with something more specific, I doubt that they will pay much attention to us. We have time to go back and snoop around more closely tomorrow. In the meantime, let's make a complete list of the missing artwork and see if there's any pattern in what they're stealing."

Neither of the boys heard Andy's dad enter the room behind them as they labored over the computer. Martin Carver watched with pride as his son and nephew methodically sorted though the police data and organized it on a spread sheet. Dates, places, types of artwork, estimated values...each found a place in the myriad of rectangles on the computer screen. Patterns *were* beginning to emerge.

"What are you learning?" asked Mr. Carver. Startled, Dave and Andy spun in their chairs to discover their unexpected visitor. The stack of printouts slid in a cascade to the floor.

"Whew!" gasped Dave, as he dropped to his knees to collect the jumble of paper. "We had no idea that you were there. It gave us a jolt!"

"That's obvious. How come you fellows are so jumpy?"

A furtive glance passed between the boys. Martin caught it. "Okay, you two. Out with it. There's more to your interest in this case than you've told us or the police."

Andy spoke first. "We took the ATVs to Killigan's Gorge to check up on something we spotted last night..."

"You're talking about the mysterious headlights?" interrupted Mr. Carver.

Andy's eyes grew wide with surprise. "How'd you know that?"

"Dave told me, after finding out that Lieutenant Parker had spotted the report on your call to the station last night. He said a chopper was sent to check out your story. The report showed that no vehicle was spotted on the ledge or down in the gorge. I was passing your room when I heard Dave mention a connection between the headlights and the robbery. What's that all about?"

Dave cleared his throat to silence Andy's next remark. "We haven't formed any conclusions, but we wondered why someone would be roaming around in the dark near the gorge and why they would suddenly disappear. I guess it's our overactive imaginations that want to tie that to the robberies."

"Dave's right," chimed in Andy. "We think there might be a hiding place near Stockbridge where the thieves take the artwork until it can be sold or smuggled out of the country. According to these reports," Andy continued, pointing at the stack of paper, "the police road-blocked the main highways after the Miller Galleries robbery and nothing appears to have left town. So—all of the stolen goods must still be around here somewhere."

"Bottom line is, though, you haven't found anything to substantiate your theory. Right?"

Dave and Andy quietly nodded.

"I'm going down to read the paper. If you boys discover anything, let me know. Okay?"

"You bet, Dad."

Martin Carver grinned and ruffled his hand through Andy's hair, throwing his locks into a tangle.

"Aw, guys! Can't you and Dave knock off messing with my hair? If any of the girls discover the disrespect you show to my crowning glory, they'll…"

He never finished the sentence because both Dave and Martin had wrestled him to the floor and were doing a truly thorough job of disrespecting his crowning glory.

After Mr. Carver left the room, the cousins returned to the spread sheet on the screen. As Andy continued to enter the report data, a low whistle escaped Dave's lips.

"Whew! Can you believe the figure in that total value column?"

"Nearly ten and a half-million dollars in stolen art?" exclaimed Andy.

Dave pointed to the top and then to the bottom entries on the date column. "All within a six-month period."

"And there could be even more than this report shows," added Andy. "Some of it might not have been discovered or reported as yet. Chances are there were more than a few unlisted robberies that took place within the same time period. That would make the evidence for a Stockbridge connection even stronger."

"That's good thinking," enthused Dave. "We can also use a spreadsheet to track the types of art taken and see how the dates match up with the different areas hit by the robbers. If we find that multiple robberies in widely scattered locations took place on the same date, we'll know that there is more than one team of thieves working at the same time."

Andy thumped the stack of reports. "It's amazing how the computer can take so many unrelated facts and tie them together. Did you see anything on the hydraulic fluid analysis in here?"

"No, but I'll check while you finish with the last few entries."

Dave soon found the analysis on the several stains found at robbery scenes. He compared the reports. They were identical except for one that appeared to have traces of jet fuel mixed in it. A grin lit Dave's face as he showed the report to his cousin.

"The list of mysteries keeps growing: stolen artwork, hydraulic fluid stains, the old church, weird tire tracks, disappearing headlights, and, now, jet fuel. Maybe we can even connect that wild jet jockey in this."

"You mean the small Lear that we spotted while on the plateau? The one you think might have been the plane that collided with your airplane the other day?"

"Right! What better way to smuggle art out of the country than by private jet?"

Andy's reply was thoughtful. "Maybe, but I think that would be awfully risky. Besides, what makes you think it's leaving the States?"

"Elementary, my dear Private Eye. The publicity about all these robberies would make it difficult to fence the goods in the States. Stockbridge is near enough to the Gulf to fly into Mexico if you have wing-tip fuel tanks like that jet had, and customs agents inspect planes coming into the US, but would have no reason to check those going out."

"You may have something, Dave," said Andy, "but I'll bet there's a lot more to the story than meets the eye. There's too much artwork missing to depend on one small plane to smuggle it all out. Nevertheless, it's worth an investigation. The question for right now is, how are we going to check out the source of the hydraulic fluid stains?"

"Remember the folks we met at the refinery last year when we helped them recover their barge?" ask Dave, referring to their exciting adventure on Sea Gate Island. "Well, I had the chance to talk with one of their lab technicians, and he gave me his card. It's in my pocket calendar."

He crossed the room and fished the leather book out of the drawer. Moments later, he shoved the cardboard rectangle with the familiar Greenfield logo under his cousins' nose. There was a home number scribbled on the back.

Dave glanced at his watch. "It's almost eleven back there, but I'll bet he's up watching the news. Will your folks mind if I call him?"

"Not as long as we're trying to get to the bottom of this mystery," declared Andy.

The technician answered on the third ring, glad to hear from his young friend.

"What can I do to be of help?"

Dave explained the events of the past few days which had led to the discovery of the stains. He read the analysis to the oil man and was put on hold for a few minutes. The line clicked, and the man explained that he had gone to collect a book on hydraulic fluids from his own library.

There were sounds of turning pages, and then..."Ah, here we are. Yes...hmmm...yes, indeed. According to the standards manual, that particular fluid is a military formula used in large ground-based hydraulic systems."

"Like what?" asked Dave.

"Like cylinders on bulldozers, large guns, canon shell elevators...that sort of thing."

"You're sure it's military?"

"Absolutely. The identification is certain if your analysis is correct. It's military."

Dave thanked him, and broke the connection. Andy had heard the whole thing on an extension phone. "Oh, great," he moaned in disappointment. "There's not a military base anywhere near here, and the stains were fresh. What kind of clue is that?"

"I'd say the best. When we find matching fluid—and we will—there won't be any question as to where the tracks came from. I think the church deserves a second visit, don't you?"

His younger cousin's face reflected the doubt in his mind. "What about those shots fired at us? You said you didn't think that it was than a careless hunter after all. What if it was one of the thief ring's vehicles whose headlights we saw? And now you're saying we may have to worry about a gang rich enough to own a jet plane."

"Humph! Some private eye you'll make. I remember when we solved the mystery of SeaGate Island, you were right in the midst of the action."

"Not by any choice of mine. In case you forgot, I was kidnapped."

Dave shrugged. "Whatever. Anyhow, it's too late to do anything about it tonight. The sun will make everything less spooky, you'll see."

Although Andy wasn't convinced he was secretly excited about learning the secrets of the shepherd's church.

He planted his fingers on his keyboard, closed his files, and shut the computer down for the night.

CHAPTER VII
The Mystery Van

Dawn did not break the next day—it exploded! A tremendous crashing of thunder and strobe-like flashes of lightning jolted the boys from their sound sleep. Andy shook the fuzziness from his head as he felt his way to the window then peered between the slats. The sky was dark with ominous, smoky clouds swirling like angry pinwheels above the mountains. Fiery discharges in the millions of volts lit up the insides of the boiling formations. Jagged streaks of lightning on the outside of the clouds appeared to hem them all together in a crazy quilt pattern.

The full storm had not yet arrived, but the guttural warnings that echoed from the mountainsides signaled a serious downpour in the vicinity of the gorge. The Carvers' outdoor plans for the day might end before they began. Even if they stayed inside, Dave worried that their computer work would be delayed since they would have to unplug everything to prevent electrical damage. He voiced his concerns to Andy.

"Hey, not to worry," declared Andy. "My whole system is protected by the UPS."

"UPS? I don't get it," said Dave. "What's a package delivery service got to do with protecting your workstation?"

"Not that United Parcel Service. I mean that I have everything plugged into an Uninterruptible Power Supply. If lightning strikes our power line, the built-in surge protector would shield my computer from damage."

"I knew that," kidded Dave.

Andy gave him a *Yeah, right!* frown and continued. "A UPS has a battery that can carry the whole system for up to twenty minutes in the event of power failure. It beeps to let you know the electricity is off, automatically saves all your open files, and then safely shuts everything down. If the line is hit really bad, the UPS takes the hit, but it's a lot cheaper than replacing the computer, not to mention all your records."

After breakfast the boys returned to Andy's room where Dave found himself staring over Andy's shoulder at the storm clouds in the distance. A small, but promising, shaft of sun had broken through and was lighting up the meadow near the old church. Both boys watched silently as the beam marched toward the building, spotlighting it in bright gold as it passed over the steeple. The swiftness of its journey showed that the hole in the clouds was being propelled at a good clip. Maybe the storm would not settle into the area after all.

"Wonder if the light on the church was some kind of sign for us to visit it?" mused Andy, aloud.

"That depends on whether or not the sky clears and we are able to get up there," said Dave, with his fingers crossed. He'd rather face the unknown at the church than sit in a room all day while any remaining signs were washed from the trail by the rain.

"Tell you what," suggested Andy. "Let's grab a quick breakfast out on the back deck and keep an eye on the weather. If it appears that it'll pass over, we'll make a fast run up there. But if that cloud snags on the peak and decides to rain on our parade, then we'll work on the spreadsheet. Either way, we can move ahead on our case."

"Whoa, cousin. Since when are we calling it *our* case? No one hired the Carver PI's to take over."

"Aw, you know what I mean, Dave. The Lieutenant *is* sharing data with us, and *is* waiting for our results. Doesn't that make us sort of Honorary Detective partners with the police? And—by the way, I couldn't help but notice how easily you let the phrase 'Carver PI' roll off your tongue."

"You win," laughed his older cousin. "I admit it does sound kinda nice." He stretched his arms out in front, palms outward, as if framing an imaginary sign with his fingers. "I can see it all now—C*arver Private Investigators, David Carver, President.*"

"Hey, this whole thing was my idea," protested Andy. "What's my title?"

"Why, Junior Assistant to the President, of course."

Andy swung at him with a pillow from the bed, but was much too late. By the time the deadly missile had passed through the space formerly occupied by his cousin's head, Dave had already bolted out of the bedroom and was heading for the kitchen.

"Too slow," shouted the escapee over his shoulder. "That's why I'm President, and you're not."

The hot chocolate felt good in the chilly breeze that swept across the deck. Rain was falling on several areas of the slope, but not in the vicinity of the path they were planning to travel. Andy was crouched near a scanner that was broadcasting the aviation and meteorology traffic from the airport. He switched it off as Dave joined him on the deck.

"The tower reports broken clouds at four-thousand and clearing conditions over Carson. That's a small town about ten miles west of here. Sounds like it'll break up shortly. We should be able to do our detective work out of doors after all."

"Great!" said Dave, affecting a cowboy twang and hooking his thumbs over his belt. "Let's get these dishes in the washer, partner, grab a sack full of snacks, and throw a saddle over our faithful ol' iron ponies. We can be at the church inside forty-five minutes if we get started now."

Suddenly, Andy grabbed Dave's arm and pointed up towards the old church. At first, Dave couldn't make out what his cousin was trying to show him. Then he saw it. A dark green extended van was parked near the end with the steeple. Unfortunately the telescope was up in the bedroom.

82

Without it, the boys couldn't make out the license plate or see who was behind the wheel.

As they watched, it pulled away from the building and headed toward the winding road leading down to Stockbridge. Although nothing conclusive could be drawn from the sighting, it did seem like a lot of loose ends were beginning to tie together. First were the mystery headlights near the gorge, followed by the shots fired at them at the church, and then finding the gas cap shortly before spotting a similar green van missing its cap at the Winn-Dixie store.

"Let's try to catch up to the van before it reaches the bottom of the mountain," urged Andy. He was turning as he spoke, but found the deck empty. Dave was already on the run to the ATVs in the barn. Andy vaulted over the rail and caught up with his cousin. They arrived at the bright red four-wheelers at the same time. Like members of a drill team, they mounted their vehicles, pulled on their helmets, switched on the intercoms, and mashed the starter buttons in unison.

"You lead," shouted Dave. The husky roar of the two-cycle engines drowned out Andy's reply. Spouting rooster tails of dirt and gravel, the ATVs fishtailed around the building and down the path that would carry them across the valley. The boys were banking on the van taking the hairpin curves at a cautious pace. That would give them time to intercept it in a wooded area just outside of town.

It was a close race, and they had only minutes to spare. For no sooner had they hid their vehicles behind a growth of brambles than the van rounded a far-off curve. As it neared, they could see that the windshield, as well as the side windows, was heavily tinted. There would be no way to identify the driver except by tailing him to his destination without being seen. They watched him go by, prepared to copy down his license number.

"Oh, no," cried Dave over the headsets. "He's got a hand-lettered sign taped on the back that claims his license plate was stolen."

"Yeah, I'll bet it was," snorted Andy. "When he's not on some secret run, he probably peels off the sign and has the real plates underneath."

Dave pointed at the side of the van. "But look—his gas cap is missing." He instinctively touched the bulk in his jacket pocket where the chrome cap from the gorge rested.

Tightening his helmet strap, Andy eased out and dodged his way between the brush and trees that paralleled the roadside, keeping the van in sight while trying not to be seen himself.

By prior agreement, Dave took a short cut through a picnic ground to leapfrog ahead to where they were certain their target would pass. The hunch was right. Andy heard Dave's voice on his helmet headset, reporting that the van was rolling along the main road toward the center of Stockbridge.

Andy took shortcuts through alleys and back streets to arrive in the Winn-Dixie parking lot before the van. He watched it stop at the gas station opposite the store and then keyed his microphone.

"We were right, Dave. He must live near here since we first saw the van in front of the grocery. He's refueling across the street. I'll watch in which direction he goes after filling up, and follow him if he heads east or west. You move down a parallel street in case he turns south."

"Roger," came the reply.

The driver, who wore a cowboy hat and dark glasses, was not familiar to Andy. The man disappeared inside to pay for the gas, then returned with a small box in his hand. He discarded the box in a trash receptacle removing a new gas cap to replace his missing one. The man glanced around, climbed into the driver's seat, shifted into gear, and aimed the van—*directly towards Andy*. The big engine propelled the van across the sidewalk. The man's intention to run him down was unmistakable.

Andy twisted the throttle, and then wrenched the handlebars around in a tight turn. The ATVs tires smoked at the unexpected maneuver, and the whining exhaust played a desperate duet with the roar of the large bore V-8. Squeaking between two parked cars, Andy bought time as the murderous pursuer had to make an end run around the lane. Andy headed straight for the drainage ditch at one side of the lot. His sure-footed four-wheeler swooped down one side and up the other.

The van driver would never be able to catch the spunky little machine, but the idea appeared to be to only scare Andy away from tailing him. He jerked the van around, and, with spinning, smoking tires, turned left at the far end of the strip mall. In seconds he had disappeared through the back entrance drive and blended into the street traffic. Andy had lost him!

Dave arrived a few minutes later, to find his dejected cousin staring morosely at the ground. The whole scenario had been reported to Dave via the radio.

"Look, Andy, it wasn't your fault. You realize that he could have been the one who took those potshots at us at the church and maybe that's how he recognized our four-wheelers."

Andy nodded glumly, then grinned. "I remember something. If this is the same van we saw here yesterday, I still have his real license that I copied down. It's on the back of my computer disk receipt back at the house."

"Great! Well, one thing's certain—if he's holed up right now in Stockbridge, then the coast should be clear for us to visit the church. We'll have to be careful, though. If he has buddies up there, he might spot us leaving and alert them."

"Not a problem," offered Andy. "I know a back way that will take care of that."

The boys, in their grim determination to solve the robberies, failed to see the van parked on an access road high above them, its tinted window rolled part way down. The driver's face was hidden by his hat and by the powerful binoculars through which he was studying his recent pursuers. As the Carvers started for the mountains, the driver pressed an auto-dial button on his cellular phone and raised the handset to his ear.

CHAPTER VIII
Caught In A Trap

True to his word, Andy wove through the back streets and alleys toward the high meadow. Dave, having become an accomplished rider himself, followed so closely that he appeared to be connected by towrope to Andy's four-wheeler. Both boys constantly scanned every parking lot and side street, hunting for the murderous van. Without being spotted by the boys, Cowboy watched their progress from his elevated hiding place. When it became obvious that they were headed for the church, he turned the ignition key and the healthy engine rumbled into life.

The Carvers stayed close to the tree line at the edge of the meadow, slipping through narrow fence openings and crossing over the metal pipes which had kept the sheep from leaving the field. Upon reaching the road, they were in wide-open country and had no choice but to make straight for the church. They could see the old building, and there was no sign of anyone, bad guys or otherwise, being there.

Andy pointed to the right of the church and spoke into his helmet mike. "Let's swing around past the church to the stand of trees behind that old barn up the road. We can act like we're heading farther up the mountain in case anyone's watching. After we hide the ATVs there, we work our way through the tall grass back to the church. Okay?"

"Sounds like a plan to me," agreed Dave.

The barn was at least a half-mile past their objective, and the upward trail curved past the far side. They concealed their mounts off the road by piling brush and leaves over them. Keeping low in the overgrown and neglected field, they crept around the opposite side of the barn and began the laborious trek back to their target.

Dave and Andy lay on their stomachs in the grass and peered through the fence at the church directly across the road from their hiding place. Nothing was moving. There was no sign of smoke or sounds coming from the building.

"So, how do you propose we cross the road without being seen?" whispered Dave.

"Well, we can't wait for dark, but there doesn't appear to be anyone there right now. Why not just walk over? If someone does show up, we can always run back into the field. You could hide an army in this grass..."

Andy was cut off in mid-sentence by the sound of an engine. Moments later, the green van rounded the bend, stirring up a dusty brown tornado behind it. It skidded sharply into a turn directly in front of the boys, and barreled up the dirt driveway leading to the church. A heavy fiber mat, attached to the rear bumper by chains, was being pulled along the ground to sweep away any tracks. Andy and Dave were seized with fits of coughing as the spinning wheels propelled a cloud of choking dust directly into their eyes and noses.

"We were right about dragging something behind them to hide their tire tracks," said Andy, between bouts of coughing.

It was several minutes before they could clear their eyes and lungs. They heard the van door slam, followed by the opening and closing of the church door. Fortunately their avenue of approach to the building was hidden by the van, which also blocked any view from inside the ruined stained glass windows.

Staying low and moving quickly, they scurried under the fence where the land had eroded away into the drainage ditch. Running in a crouch, they reached the side of the van and eased around the rear bumper. Dave signaled that they were well past any sight line from the inside of the building. He indicated that they could run for the near side by keeping below the window line.

"Ready? On my count of three," whispered Dave. "One, two, thr…"

Andy was already hugging the siding under the middle window, one of the few not yet broken by vandals. Dave frowned at his younger cousins' lack of caution, but then quickly joined him. They crept along the side to where they had heard the rumbling of a large engine inside the church on their last visit.

Dave tapped Andy's arm and pointed above his cousin's head. Two large round bullet holes six feet above

90

the ground were evidence of how close a call they had had from the shots fired at them the day before.

The sound of arguing voices filtered through the jagged holes in the next window as they crept forward. Andy, much to Dave's nervous concern, stood up to peek inside. He quickly stooped down and placed his mouth near the older Carver's ear.

"The voices are coming from behind a door near the old choir loft," he said. "Sounds like two men arguing."

They silently belly-crawled to the farthest window, which no longer contained any of its inspiring stained-glass images. The angry conversation was stronger now.

"You are a stupid fool, Cowboy. How could you let them see you?" demanded the one who seemed to be in charge.

"Hey, I covered over the van's license plate to keep anyone from tracing me. I was just trying to scare them off," said the man in the cowboy hat.

"You were ordered to keep a low profile. If those snooping kids get more looks at us, they'll be in our backyard and we'll be in the dumps."

"Aw, come off it, Blake. We'll all be out of here in a week or so, and you'll be rich enough to retire anywhere you want. Quit being so serious."

"Somebody better be serious. It's obvious that you aren't. What are you doing up here at this hour, anyway? Your delivery isn't scheduled until after ten tonight."

Cowboy fell into an old chair left behind by the vandals who had sacked the abandoned church over the years. The few remaining pieces were not worth stealing. He grunted as a broken spring poked the back of his leg. Gingerly rubbing the spot, he was surprised to discover that it was bleeding.

"That's all I need. Look at my leg—this stupid chair stabbed me. You got some bandages?"

"Later! I asked why you came here in the daylight."

"Look, Blake, the kids were tailing me. I gave them the slip and then followed them. I saw them headed up this way and came to make sure they weren't coming here."

"Well?"

"Didn't see them. They probably went up into the snow line again."

"Forget the kids. I've been given orders to have them and their four-wheelers taken care of. Now you get off this mountain before someone else sees you. And steal another van—that one out there's been compromised."

Cowboy got slowly to his feet and began limping for the door, muttering to himself.

Outside, Andy moved close to Dave. "So much for learning the driver's name from the license number if the vehicle's stolen. That bossy character said they'll be after us and our four-wheelers, and the one called Cowboy is heading out to the van. We'd better get out of sight behind the church."

Dave nodded, and they both started crawling on hands and knees toward shelter. Andy didn't notice the broken glass on the ground until his hand found it.

"Ouch!" he involuntarily exclaimed. Inside, there was a sudden rush of footsteps to the window above him. Though both Carvers had begun to run, it was too late. Cowboy spotted them when he leaned out of the broken window.

"It's those lousy brats. They were outside the window and must've been listening to us. I watched them running for the back of the church. Better call the guys."

Blake grabbed the radio and issued orders. The voice on the other end acknowledged, and moments later there was the sound of a gasoline engine being started beneath the steeple.

Dave and Andy were close to the structure and heard the rumble of the exhaust. From the belfry came the squeal of a pulley badly in need of lubrication.

"What's that, Dave?"

"My guess is that it's some kind of lift or elevator, but that makes no sense. The church is a one-story building."

Then the front door of the church banged open at moments after the noisy pulley groaned to a stop. Shouts, banging of a door, then running feet. Suddenly, there were more than the two men Andy had seen through the window.

The Carvers scrambled around the corner at the rear of the church, frantically searching for the nearest place to hide. Dave pointed to a small building about twenty feet away near the edge of the woods.

"Run for the back of that shed as fast as you can run," he urged. "Duck into the woods and make your way toward the barn where we hid the four-wheelers. I'll be there in a moment."

"Dave, they'll catch you. We need to stay together!" Andy grabbed Dave's shirt and began tugging him toward safety, but the older Carver slapped his hand away and gave him a push toward the shed.

Not understanding, but knowing that his cousin must have a plan and that time was running out, Andy did as ordered. Dave sprinted to the fuel tank and quickly opened a drain valve on one end. The volatile fluid poured out in an amber stream filling the air with the unmistakable odor of gasoline. He groped in his pockets and found what he hoped would be there.

Cowboy limped around the corner, followed quickly by Blake and the three men who had mysteriously appeared from the interior of the church. All but one had handguns. The fifth man's weapon was a double-barreled shotgun. They halted in shock, nearly bowling one another over. Dave stood next to the growing puddle of fuel, his hand held out in front of him holding a cigarette lighter.

"The kid's crazy! He'll blow us all to bits."

"He's bluffin'," shouted Cowboy, but his voice betrayed his lack of conviction. "He wouldn't dare. He'd be the first one to go up. You men go get him and the other brat before they get away and bring the Feds down on us."

"Don't take another step," shouted Dave. "Whatever you guys are up to is none of our business. We'll go away and forget we've even seen anyone up here."

Blake moved to the front of the group and snarled, "You cowards grab him, or you'll all be doing hard time the rest of your lives."

A spark appeared in Dave's hand, and he began to lean down toward the escaping gasoline. It was every man for himself as the five crooks scrambled over each other in their haste to put distance between them and the impending explosion. Dave bolted in the opposite direction. Seconds later, he was flailing through the woods toward his rendezvous with Andy. He finally reached the barn and fell panting over a pile of straw in the decaying structure. Panting for air, he didn't hear the approach of footsteps until a hand clamped on his shoulder. Rolling over on his back, Dave doubled up his legs, ready to deliver a hammer blow with his feet to the stomach of his captor.

"Stop! It's me," hissed Andy. "The ATVs are outside. Let's split before they get here." The advice was good, but their timing was not. Outside, they could hear the familiar roar of the van racing up the road toward them. Before Andy could help Dave to his feet, the van skidded to a halt, the side doors already slid open. Suddenly, five angry men blocked both exits from the barn.

CHAPTER IX
The Secret Mine Shaft

Dave was unceremoniously jerked to his feet by one of the thugs, while Andy's arm was grabbed by another and bent behind him in a hammerlock. They were shoved though the door and then sent stumbling into the van. Two of their captors mounted the boys' four-wheelers, and the caravan of vehicles headed back toward the church.

Blake, sitting in the passenger seat of the van, turned to glare at Dave who was sandwiched between two of the men. "You stupid or something, kid? You coulda' blown all of us to kingdom come, including yourself, with that fool trick."

"What's he talking about?" asked Andy.

"After I knew you had gotten safely away," explained Dave, "I opened the drain valve on the fuel tank behind the church and flooded the area with gasoline."

"Yeah, then your smart friend threatened to set it off with his cigarette lighter," growled Blake.

"You what?" exploded Andy. "Why would you take a chance like that...? Wait a minute. Since when have you carried a lighter?"

Dave gave his younger cousin a wry smile. "I had to take a chance like that to give you and me a time to get away from these thieving crooks, but..."

One of Dave's guards elbowed him in the ribs for the unflattering comment.

Grimacing with the sudden pain, Dave continued, "As I was about to say, it wasn't that big of a chance. Here's my 'cigarette lighter.' " He fished a small pencil flashlight out of his pocket. "I switched this on while leaning down and let their imagination do the rest."

"Okay, kid, I'll give you credit...you fooled us that one time," said Blake. "But as you can clearly see, you're not about to have the last laugh. Now you two sit still and shut up until I tell you differently!" To emphasize the point, he pulled a lethal-looking snub-nose revolver from his shirtfront.

The van rolled into the parking lot at the front of the old church. The cousins were roughly prodded up the worn steps and propelled through the still-open doors. Cowboy limped along behind, the deep puncture wound in his leg beginning to grow more painful. He tried to shrug it off, but the worry of a serious infection from the rusty chair spring was affecting his concentration.

"Come-on," snorted Blake, his exasperation obvious in his tone. "The Priest'll have to decide what to do with these punk kids now that you've brought them here." Dave sneaked a glance at Andy; a questioning look in his eyes. What did a priest have to do with all of this?

"I didn't have a thing to do with bringing them here," protested Cowboy. "They must have already been at the church when I pulled up. It was the boss's dumb idea in the first place to set up smuggling operations in a building that can be seen for miles around!"

Blake, obviously the one in charge, turned and struck Cowboy across the face.

"Shut your mouth, you scatter-brained idiot. Your loose tongue'll do more damage than that tank of gas would have done if the kid had used a real lighter. Take them down to the storage room. The Priest gave orders for us to dump them into the Gulf, but he wants to see them first."

Cowboy, still glaring, removed his hand from a reddened cheek. "Don't you ever hit me again." Glancing at the two uneasy boys, he turned back to face Blake, his voice less hostile. "You aren't serious about us following orders to kill them, are you? I don't want anything to do with murder. Especially killing a kid belonging to one of the town's top businessmen."

"Well, then, why don't you go tell our boss, the good *Priest,* how you feel about it, hmm?"

A brilliant flash of lightning and ear-shattering crash of thunder interrupted Blake's response. Another fierce downpour was about to drench the meadow, adding to the rain-swollen river surging through the gorge.

Cowboy yelled at the men who were still standing around, and jerked his head toward the Dave and Andy, who were then herded up the steps of the pulpit platform and into the choir loft. A wide section of dummy organ pipes swung out on well-oiled hinges. Behind it was hidden a freight elevator big enough to hold the five crooks and their two captives with plenty of room to spare. When Blake touched a button on the panel next to the door, the loud rumble of a large engine starting up drowned out any communication.

Closing the organ pipes and elevator door behind him, Blake moved a lever on the side of the car and it began to slowly descend. The shaft was cut though solid rock, and they passed through strata that recorded perhaps millions of years of history. The boys would have been fascinated by their journey through time if things had been different, but they were understandably absorbed by the danger in which they found themselves.

Several hundred feet below the church, the elevator car ground to a halt. With the touch of another button the nearby sound of the engine died away, although a more distant hum signaled the presence of a large generator. No one spoke as the door opened. The crooks with their two prisoners moved out into a well-lit hallway. The walls were coated with a moisture sealer, as was the stone floor, worn smooth by decades of traffic.

Andy wondered if this could be the lost Killigan mine. His deduction was strengthened when they reached a cross-tunnel where a narrow-gauge rail lay partially buried under the packed earth. He lightly bumped against his cousin's shoulder, and then glanced toward the floor. Dave acknowledged his discovery with a small nod.

They reached a section of tunnel where the soil was still loose enough to show footprints—and something else. There were knobby tire tracks like those made by their own ATVs, and there were also narrower ones made by tires with straight treads like those found on a trailer. After ten minutes of walking, they arrived at what appeared to be a dead-end to the tunnel. The tire tracks swerved left and ended at a solid wall. The boys were jerked to a stop as the crooks waited for Cowboy and Blake to catch up.

Their leader reached behind a rock outcropping and pressed a hidden switch. The sidewall of the tunnel began to swing away from them, revealing a huge cavern, brightly lit, and populated with several dozen men. It was like an underground factory with a number of work areas and several small buildings that resembled prefabricated supervisors' offices.

A pair of ATVs with trailers was parked near the center. One trailer was filled with framed paintings covered over with clear plastic. The Carvers had been right. This *was* the headquarters for the art-theft ring.

The mystery was how they had managed to bring all of the equipment and furnishings into the mine without being noticed by the townspeople. Even more disturbing was the fact that they were also getting past everyone with load after load of stolen artwork.

The workers were obviously curious about the two young prisoners, but were fearful of being seen to show any interest. Dave wondered what kind of hold Blake and this strange Priest guy had on them.

Two of the men returned to whatever they had been doing before being interrupted to help capture the cousins. Cowboy and Blake prodded the boys onward toward metal stairs at the far end of the cavern. Dave was the first to notice the easels set up in a brightly lit alcove where the more valuable paintings were being copied. Andy followed Dave's gaze and quickly understood what was going on. Cowboy clouted him on the cheek from behind to force his eyes to the front.

Dave, angered by the treatment of his younger cousin, half-turned and delivered a karate kick to Cowboy's thigh. It was the same leg that was causing even more agonizing pain from the growing infection. The man howled in shock and surprise. He clutched at his wounded limb as he crashed to the floor.

Blake raised his pistol and would have shot Dave except for the quiet but chilling voice that came from the doorway at the top of the stairs.

"Pull that trigger and you're a dead man, Mr. Blake!"

Blake turned his head and glared into the dark eyes of the one he had called the Priest, and then defiantly turned back to where Dave stood with clenched fists over the downed crook. Blake took a step forward, brought the butt of the pistol down on the back of the young man's head, and watched him collapse in a heap. There was an audible gasp from several of the guards standing nearby.

"Bring both of them up here," snapped the Priest. "I promise you, if he dies, you join him," he said to Blake. "You men, give them a hand, and then all of you get back up to the church and set up a guard around the perimeter until you're relieved."

Remembering the warning issued by the man on the stairs, the guards handled Dave and Andy almost gently. Still unconscious, the older Carver was laid on the couch. Cowboy was helped into a reclining chair where his injured leg could be elevated. The mysterious man in priestly garments knelt by Dave and began to treat the head wound administered by his rebellious lieutenant.

Forgetting the dangerous situation he was in, Andy found himself aiding the Priest by handing him moist cloths, ointment, and bandages. It was a strange mixture of cruelty and compassion that he witnessed in the man. Who was he, and why was he masquerading as a man of the cloth? Was *he* the head of this crime organization, or were there more above him?

Andy shivered as he realized that this man tending his cousin was apparently the same person who had told Blake and Cowboy to dump Dave and him into the Gulf. That must mean they intended to take them aboard a ship—make them walk the plank, so to speak. At least that would give them some time to plan an escape, or even rig some way to stay afloat until they could be found.

His small glimmer of hope would have faded in a heartbeat had he known that the plank they were to walk was not from aboard a floating ship, but rather from a jet airplane several thousand feet above the Gulf of Mexico.

CHAPTER X
A Long Way Down

Andy sat on the floor, his head resting against the couch. He was instantly alert when he felt Dave stir and softly moan. The Priest looked up from his paperwork, and then crossed the room from behind his desk. He removed the damp cloth from his patient's forehead, refreshed it with clean water, and, after wringing out the excess moisture, began to bathe Dave's face.

The older Carver opened his eyes at the shock of the cool cloth, then narrowed them at the sight of the man in cleric's frock and collar who was tending to him. "What's happening to me? Who are you? Where's my cousin? I want to see Andy!"

Andy rose to his knees and leaned over to peer into Dave's eyes. They seemed to react normally enough. At least he didn't appear to have had a concussion. "Easy, Dave. I'm right here, and I'm fine. How does your head feel?"

"Like an anvil fell on it. Did I fall down the stairs?'

Blake moved in closer, a cruel smile pasted across his face. "Try a .38 caliber anvil, kid. But trust me, a fall down the stairs would be a walk in the park compared to what's coming up for you and your nosy friend."

The Priest grabbed his arm and spun him around. "This is the last time I warn you, Blake. Keep your mouth shut and do what you're told. I won't stand for your rebellious actions another time. Cowboy, get on the P.A. system. Have two of the guards take these boys to the vault. They're to have water, sandwiches, and blankets. If Blake disobeys my orders again, you see that he's tied up and put in with them—only without food, water, and blankets. Is that clear?"

"Yessir," Cowboy quickly acknowledged. "Does this mean I'm in charge now?"

The man in clerical robes stopped behind his desk—anger flashed in his eyes. His normally quiet voice roared. "*I'M* the one in charge! I've *ALWAYS BEEN* the one in charge! I'll *ALWAYS BE* the one in charge. Now—*GET OUT!!*"

The guards rushed to the office door, hesitant to enter at the ominous sound of their leader's angry voice. Then Cowboy yanked open the door and impatiently gestured the men inside. "Take the kids down to the art vault. See that they have water, sandwiches, and blankets. They're not stupid, so make sure you lock them in. And leave the lights on so we can watch them on the security camera."

The vault had ben installed at the end of a long sloping passage that opened near the bottom of the office stairs. As the boys and their captors moved along toward the great steel door, they passed the mouth of a branch tunnel off to the side. Dave automatically noted landmark features near it and began counting steps from that point to where they were being taken.

It was uncomfortably cool and dry in the vault that was designed to protect the stolen artwork. Dave and Andy huddled together, wrapped in blankets, and ate their meal as if it were their last. Realizing that they had been witness to a criminal operation unknown to any of the law officials working on the case, it was plain to see that they would not be allowed to get out of here—at least not while they were alive.

Andy shivered—only partly from the cold. "Dave, they mean to kill us. Blake is crazy. I don't think he's kidding about throwing us off a ship in the Gulf. I'm scared, and you know I don't scare easily."

"Yeah, well, don't feel you're alone. My head hurts so bad that I can't think clearly. There doesn't seem to be any way for us to get out of this mess. We're locked in a vault hundreds of feet underground, surrounded by a gang of thieves, forgers, and kidnappers. Nevertheless, we have to work together to find a way to escape."

Andy leaned close to his ear. "There's a camera up in the corner behind you. I bet there's also a microphone." While he whispered, he appeared to anybody watching him on a monitor to be just doodling in the dust. In reality, he was scratching a diagram of the passageway showing the side tunnel. Dave could see it, but the drawing was hidden from the camera. He nodded almost imperceptibly.

The boys ate their sandwiches in deep thought, as they worked on a plan of escape. Dave traced several words on the floor and then carefully rubbed out the drawing and writing.

"We might be able to find out if they're listening," whispered the older cousin. "Follow my lead."

In a normal voice, he said to Andy. "I wouldn't get too worried. Lieutenant Parker will soon discover our voice mail message about the green van and the church. He and his squad should be here within minutes after your parents report us missing. They'll find that elevator in the church right where we said it would be. Trust me, it'll only be a matter of time before they find us down here."

Andy brightened, making sure the camera in the corner caught his confident expression. "That's right. I had forgotten about that! Blake, Cowboy, and that fake priest are about to get the surprise of their lives."

The boys seemed to be chuckling about their impending rescue, but were, in reality, enjoying their bluff. If there *were* hidden microphones, the reaction would be coming in short order.

It did.

The vault reverberated with the sounds of tumblers moving behind the steel panel. Then the door swung open noiselessly on massive hinges. The same guards that brought them, pulled them to their feet, threw their blankets in the corner, and shoved the Carvers out ahead of them.

Both boys knew there would be no more "Mr. Nice Guy" from the leader of crooks, now that they'd revealed themselves to be associated with the police. It was a dangerous gamble, but it might be their only chance to escape. Dave and Andy had experienced a number of close calls over the years, and instinctively knew how to follow each other's lead.

As they approached the passage they had spotted earlier, Andy suddenly clutched his stomach and doubled over. "Dave, I think the meat in that sandwich was bad. Oh, man, it hurts. I think I'm going to be sick." He staggered over to the wall, still hunched over, and started gagging.

The two guards were caught off balance. As one of the men followed after Andy, Dave delivered a roundhouse kick to the side of the second guard's stomach. He fell with a groan, striking his head against the wall as his rifle slid across the cavern floor. Dave scrambled to snatch it up, and then spun back toward the fallen man. He wasn't moving.

The first guard glanced around at the noise, and Andy charged him from behind, sending him sprawling to the hard rock. The man rolled over on his back, still gripping his weapon, but found his face just inches from Dave's rifle barrel.

"I'm an expert shot," said Dave. "Not that I'd have to be one this close to my target. Take your finger off the trigger. Lay your gun down beside you. Good. Now put your hands behind your head."

With no choice, the guard sullenly complied. Andy stooped to retrieve the second gun.

Andy questioned Dave. "What do we do with them?"

His cousin gestured toward the unconscious guard. "Pick up your friend and lead the way into the side tunnel."

The man smirked and continued to lie with his hands behind his back.

Dave pushed the barrel of his rifle into the man's ear. "Perhaps I didn't make myself clear. I'm even a better shot at zero range. And, yes, the safety is off, so move."

Andy had never heard him speak so forcefully, but then they had never been in quite the situation in which they now found themselves.

The guard deciding not to push the determined young man any further at this stage, wrestled his unconscious companion into a fireman's carry. There would be time to overcome these pushover kids. He could wait. Dave pointed to the passage, and prodded the man forward with his rifle barrel.

"Ain't no way you can get outta here," their former captor grunted under the load on his shoulder. "There's security cameras all over this place and they'll be hunting for us the minute we don't show up with you guys."

Dave's voice was grim and desperate. "If and when they find us, a lot of people will get hurt, but especially you and your friend. It would be a smart thing for you to show us how to get out of this mine and away from here."

The logic of this was not lost on the man. If his cohorts began shooting they would not hesitate to hit anyone near the boys. Despite the old saying, there really is no honor among thieves.

The guard relented. "A few yards ahead, there's an old ladder in a shaft that leads down into a lower tunnel. The river flows through it and you could swim out, but there ain't no way I can carry Ben down there. You'll have to leave me at the top."

"Nice try," said Dave with a wry smile. "We'll leave what's his name—Ben, but you go with us. If you're telling the truth, you'll be free soon enough, although I don't think your so-called 'Priest' boss will take kindly to your letting us escape. You may want to consider taking a swim to freedom with us."

At the ladder, the guard, with a sigh of relief, dumped his buddy against the wall. Andy told him to remove Ben's jacket, tie knots in the sleeves, and put it backwards on the still unconscious guard. Even if the man woke up, he would find his arms pinned inside the jacket and the zipper out of reach in back of him.

That done, Dave stooped to take Ben's flashlight from his belt clip, and then aimed it down the shaft at the corroded metal rungs. The incandescent beam faded before revealing what lay beyond the nothingness below them.

"How far down does this thing go?"

"About a hundred feet," said the guard. "It's old, and wet, and slippery. Sure you want to risk it?"

"We have no choice and neither do you. I'll go first, you follow, and Andy will stay about twenty feet above you."

Dave slung the rifle strap over his head, while his cousin continued to cover the man with the second weapon. The three moved to the ladder and Dave began the long climb downwards, feeling the dampness coating the rungs. Flakes of rust fell away under his hand, and the ladder quivered under his weight.

What would happen when all of them were on it? A shiver that traveled through his body was not the result of any shakiness of the ladder. He jammed the flashlight upright in his jacket pocket so he could keep an eye on the guard and his cousin above him. He had no desire to look down.

"Stay at least twenty feet apart so our weight will be distributed on several wall anchors," warned Dave. "If any of the bolts start pulling out of the wall this thing could tear loose, taking us with it. Let's go. The quicker we reach bottom, the better."

The trio started down as fast as they dared, maintaining space between them, and sensing every creaking groan of the weathered steel. Small pieces of rock fell continually from around the anchors holding the structure to the wall. Occasionally an entire rung would be missing.

Abruptly, there was a sharp snap. The step under the guard's foot broke loose. The sharp metal dowel struck Dave on the right hand, causing him to lose his grip on that side. He swung wildly away to the left, clinging desperately with his left hand. The violent reaction tore his feet from the slippery rungs. He found himself hanging by one hand over the black abyss.

His flashlight jolted from his pocket and plummeted away in tumbling stabs of light. The bulb shattered as it bounced off the side of the shaft and the darkness swallowed them. Several more seconds ticked away before a soft splash echoed back up to the three who held their breath in the midnight black.

The guard had recovered his footing and was now working his way down to Dave. If he could kick the boy off the ladder, he'd only have Andy to deal with, and he knew the younger boy was at the disadvantage of being above him in an unfamiliar place. He had not counted on the cool-headedness of his captors, however. When he was but a few feet above the struggling Dave, he felt the cold hard barrel of Andy's rifle against his scalp.

"Don't even think about it," came the determined sound of the voice from above. "I heard you moving faster and knew what you were thinking. Dave...are you all right?"

His cousin had managed to swing back and grasp the side of the ladder with his aching hand, then work his feet back onto solid rungs. His lungs burned from the exertion, and his voice sounded weak and far away.

"I'm all right. Let me catch my breath, and I'll put some more space between us. That should take some of the pressure off these anchor bolts."

"Count off about twenty steps, and I'll have our friend start down. Okay?"

"Right. Here I go. One...two...three...."

At twenty, Andy prodded the guard and made him count aloud, too. When another twenty steps had been counted, Andy followed. The three moved with even more caution, realizing that any of them could be the next one to lose his footing in the deep darkness. Sweaty palms made the journey more hazardous as minutes passed.

"Stop," commanded Dave. He reached into his pocket and pulled out a coin. "Listen."

The coin fell away. Almost immediately, there was a splash. They were very close to the bottom.

Dave climbed up to just below the guard, wrapped his left arm around the ladder, and aimed the rifle with his right forefinger on the trigger. "I just remembered. You have a flashlight, too. Unclip it; point the beam away from my eyes, and down to the river. Be careful. My trigger finger is extremely nervous at this point."

The man complied. Dave breathed a sigh of relief to see that a shallow ledge lay just beneath the surface of the water, which was only about ten feet below his feet. Dave moved to the bottom rung of the ladder. He eased down to hang by his hands. Taking a deep breath, he dropped into three feet of cold water. After wading to one side, Dave ordered the guard into the water. As the man splashed down on the ledge, Dave kept the rifle pointed at him and backed away along the wall, telling the man to follow. Andy dropped to the ledge taking his position behind the guard.

"That way," said their captive, gesturing toward a low and narrow tunnel. "The water level's up from all the rain. It shouldn't get any deeper, though. This stream empties into a big cave up ahead. This was an escape route in the early days of the mine in case of a cave-in or gas pockets in the main shafts."

Dave nodded, and indicated that the guard was to lead the way. He took the flashlight from the man and held it as near the top of the passage as he could. They waded nearly a hundred yards before the tunnel made a sharp bend to the right. Both Carvers drew in sharp breaths when they rounded the curve and saw lights ahead.

"What's that?" Dave whispered to the guard.

The man turned, and his face, caught in the flashlight beam, displayed a self-satisfied smile. "*That,* boys, is the end of your little adventure. It's our loading dock inside the cave for shipping out the artwork. The dock is manned by more of my friends. There's no way to get past them. Now, let me have the gun, and I'll lead you guys out. That way, there'll be no shooting and no one gets hurt." He reached for the rifle.

Dave struck his hand out of the way with the barrel. "The situation is the same. Whether you will admit it or not, we're all in the same boat. If we get hurt, you get hurt. Now move and keep quiet!" he hissed.

Andy moved up beside his cousin. "What's the plan?" he whispered.

His cousin shrugged. "I'm thinking." He moved ahead through the icy water. Nearing the light, he reached out and grabbed the guard's shirt. "Get behind me and stay put. Remember, Andy's got you covered, and he's just as desperate as I am."

"Make that twice as desperate," came the hushed comment.

Dave crouched down and waded quietly forward until he could peer further out of the opening. He was astounded at the sight of the powerful inboard boats tied up to the long wooden dock. There were also stacks of shapeless objects wrapped in waterproof tarps. To his right, a large tunnel curved away into darkness.

There was apparently no other way for the boats to come and go. That had to be an opening into the river that flowed through Killigan's Gorge. Two men were standing and talking near a freight elevator door.

Dave studied the area. He spotted two security cameras located where they could overlook the boats and cargo. The bright light came from a pair of flood lamps mounted near the cameras.

This might be their only way out of the mine, and stealing a boat was their only hope. Now, thought Dave, all we have to do is get past the men on the dock and the cameras on the wall without being seen, take one of the boats, pray that it starts, make our way out of the cave, and get to the nearest help, probably while dodging bullets.

Piece of cake!

Yeah, right.

CHAPTER XI
The Phantom Bridge

Dave retraced his way back to Andy and the guard. His feet were aching with the cold wetness that had soaked through his clothes and shoes. Never mind that, he thought—his cousin was counting on him and he had to come through.

"Okay, here's how we play it. The good news is that there are several fast-looking boats moored at a dock out there that could free us from this mess. The bad news is that there are also several men and at least two cameras covering the place. So, while you keep an eye on our friend here, I'll swim underwater to the nearest boat. If I can climb aboard and get it started, I'll swing by the tunnel and pick you up."

"What about me?" whispered their prisoner. "You're right about the gang taking your escape out on me. Besides, I know the way out of the cave. You don't."

Andy had kept silent through most of the frightening trip down the ladder and through the passageway. Now he spoke with quiet determination. "You tried to kick Dave off the ladder back there. That gives us no reason to trust you now. I say 'no' to taking you with us."

"Hey," the man objected. "Both of you were trying to escape, and you clobbered one of my friends in the process. Why do you think it's wrong when I try to fight back?"

Andy pushed his face close to the guard. "It's wrong because you're a crook—and we're not!"

Dave considered both arguments before speaking. "Look. We all have a choice to make." He pointed at the guard. "Plan one. The only way we can leave you here is to knock you out cold. That would keep you from giving us away and might even buy you some sympathy from your 'friends.' However, there's no way we can prop you up above water, so you'd probably drown.

"Andy has a point about not wanting to worry about keeping you honest while we avoid being shot or running the boat into a wall or some underwater obstacle. So here's plan two. I'm going to tie a gag over your mouth so you can't shout, then you're going to get down on your knees so only your face is above the water. You'll stay that way until I return with the boat. If you try to stand up, Andy has my permission to return to plan one. Agreed?"

The guard nodded as Andy sneaked a peek out of the passage and then quickly waded back.

Dave continued. "If anything goes wrong, Andy, you're to fire the rifle out of the opening towards the far end of the cave away from the outlet to the river. The echo should confuse the men on the dock, so they won't be able to trace the source. Once they duck for cover, I'll try for the boat. You may have to cover me with some follow-up shots. Can you handle it?"

"You bet. A few shots would sound like a whole army in here. As soon you head for this side, I'll let our crooked friend get up off his knees and climb aboard. How long he stays aboard depends on his behavior."

Dave fashioned a gag from Andy's handkerchief and the drawstring from the hood on his jacket. The cloth, rolled around the string, was placed in the guard's mouth, and the wet string was tied securely behind the man's head. The only way it could be removed would be to cut it off.

"Let's do it," said Dave, tightening the rifle strap across his shoulder as he began deep breathing before submerging. There was a large tangled clump of driftwood fifteen yards away. A thick growth of ancient stalagmites protruded above the water near the middle of the cave. If he could hold his breath long enough to reach those hiding places, they had a good chance to make it.

Giving Andy a thumbs-up, he emptied his lungs several times, took a deep breath and smoothly slipped beneath the water. Andy crossed his fingers, hoping the men on the dock would not notice the tiny wake that might betray his cousin's swim out to the driftwood.

A minute, then two, ticked away before Dave's head slowly rose above the surface. Step one—complete. Andy watched as his cousin readjusted the rifle strap and peeked around the driftwood pile toward the dock. Satisfied that the men were occupied in conversation, Dave filled his lungs and dove for the stalagmite formation.

Suddenly, there was a loud splash. The men on the dock grabbed for their rifles and searched in every direction for the cause. One of them pointed to a spreading circle of wavelets near the spot where Dave was submerged. Another man laughed and gestured to the vaulted ceiling above the disturbance. A flashlight beam aimed upwards and traced a ring of light around the broken-off stump of a stalactite. Andy caught his breath and slumped against the sidewall. He had almost fired the shot to distract them before Dave had even reached the boats. It was a close call.

With the splash explained, the men sat down on a pair of crates and lit cigarettes. Maybe this was a stroke of good luck. They might consider any other small disturbance as just another rock shower from the ceiling. That could make Dave's job much easier...and safer.

When Andy again stole a glance, Dave was already under the dock, behind the stern of the boat nearest the tunnel where Andy and the guard were hidden. Dave worked his way forward and dove beneath the next boat. Seconds later, he appeared behind the third boat, and, again, disappeared under the water.

With a deep sigh of relief, Andy finally saw Dave surface behind the middle boat, then pull himself up the stern boarding ladder. The interior of the speedy craft was below the view of the men who were lounging on some crates and couldn't see Dave as he stealthily worked his way forward to the cockpit. Staying below the dock line, he quietly removed the rifle, let the water drain from the barrel, and then placed it on the top of the dash.

The keys hung in the ignition and the fuel gauge read full, as he knew it would. The controls were normal—gear shift lever with trim control switch by his right hand, choke next to the keys, and an automotive-type floor accelerator. This baby was built to move, and fast. Smuggling required more than a Sunday cruiser to stay ahead of the law.

The boat was secured to the dock by bow and stern lines that were clipped to electrically released hooks activated from the cockpit. Nice touch for an emergency get away and if there ever was such an occasion, this was it. Dave breathed deeply, calming himself, and then gave a small wave to Andy. He still had not been sighted. Thank you, thank you!

Now or never. He carefully gripped the rifle stock, lifted it from the dash, and placed his left forefinger on the trigger. With his right hand, he pulled out the choke, released the hooks, pumped the accelerator once, and turned the key to the start position. Without hesitation, the powerful engine fired. Its throaty roar filled the cave.

The men jumped for their rifles and turned toward the boat. As soon as Dave had cleared the protection of the dock, he knew he would be met with a hail of bullets. Still, there was no going back, so he slammed the shift lever into forward and then spun the wheel to the left. As the boat lurched forward it barely missed the boat in front of him.

Andy saw the movement on the dock, then rapidly fired his own rifle above the heads of the men. When the firing pin clicked on an empty chamber, he dropped the now-useless weapon and it sank to the bottom of the river. Andy smiled with grim satisfaction as he watched the armed crooks scrambling for cover.

Dave fired several more times back over the stern, then laid his own weapon on the floor to concentrate on driving. He swept the boat in a large curving turn to make it a harder target and steered it safely around the driftwood and rock formations. Slowing and shifting into neutral, he glided close to the tunnel opening. Andy and the gagged guard were waiting for him, both of them eager to get aboard and away.

A hail of bullets slammed into the wall right above the boat. The driftwood was apparently making it difficult for men on the dock to see and hit their target.

"No time to get in right now," shouted Dave. "Both of you grab hold of a docking fender. I'll try to get us around the bend in the entrance tunnel."

The two clung to the rubber cylinders that protected the side of the boat from chaffing against the dock. Dave selected forward gear, crouched low in the boat, and began to slowly move ahead. He felt around on the floor until he regained the rifle, and then, pointing it above the general direction of the dock, he fired three rapid rounds. A hailstorm of stalactite pieces rained from the ceiling onto the dock. It was enough to keep the men down behind the crates until the boat was safely around the curve.

Andy and the guard, resembling water soaked rats, wearily pulled themselves over the side, collapsing on the deck. Dave found the spotlight switch and worked at navigating around the rocks and driftwood that dotted the way.

Andy helped the guard into the front passenger seat, and searched for something to cut off the man's gag. A fishing knife stored in a side pocket did the job of sawing through the string. Their prisoner jerked the handkerchief from his mouth and flung it over the side.

Massaging his sore lips, the guard suddenly pointed ahead and exclaimed, "There. That's the exit. Be careful, there's only one way through it."

Dave saw traces of moonlight through trees and brush. They were almost home free! He followed the man's direction, swerving this way and that until he was forced to stop a few feet from the impenetrable tangle of limbs and leaves. Behind them, he could hear the roar of another boat starting up. Andy moved to the stern and aimed Dave's rifle back along the way they had just traveled.

The guard appeared to be frantically searching around for something. He aimed the spotlight down into the water and grabbed for a paddle. Andy swung the barrel around at the noise and centered his aim on the man.

"Cover the tunnel, kid. I'm in this now as much as you are. The switch to open the entrance is hidden under water." With that, he plunged the end of the paddle between two rocks beneath the surface. The soft whir of electric motors was joined by the swish of the camouflaged gate opening outwards.

"Go, go, go!" urged the guard. Dave gladly obeyed.

The moon was almost blinding as they entered the river. Behind them, the clever weave of living plants began swinging shut again. The sound of the boat in the cave suddenly choked into silence.

"They've given up on us," said Andy.

"Not by choice," said Dave, a grin spread across his face. "When I dove under the other boats, I wrapped the props up in old nylon rope that was tied under the dock. I imagine they're completely fouled up by now."

"What now?" asked their prisoner.

"We'll let you out the first opportunity we can land, and you're on your own. If you should get caught, Andy and I promise to tell how you helped us escape from the cave."

"I have a better idea," said the man. "Why don't I let you two out, then take the boat as far as I can to draw off any of the guys who'll be after you. You know it's only a matter of time until they get one of the boat props unsnarled, and then they'll be hot on our trail. They can't afford to let you guys get back to the police."

"Nice try," said Andy. "You make a run to wherever you take the stolen art, report to your cronies that you broke away from us and send them back to hunt us down. You either accept the offer, or we turn you over to the police."

"Fair enough," he said with a smile. There's a beach where I can get out just around the next bend, and..."

"Dave!" shouted Andy, pointing up over the bow of the boat. "Look! Up there!" He gestured frantically.

His cousin throttled back the engine and let his gaze follow where Andy's waggling finger aimed up the side of the towering granite walls.

Silhouetted against the moonlight, and crossing the gorge high above the wreckage of the ancient wooden trestle in the river bed, was *a bridge that had not been there before this night.* As Dave and his younger cousin stared in stunned amazement, they saw the right side of the gorge suddenly illuminated by approaching headlights. From their vantage point hundreds of feet below, they watched as a vehicle approached and eased out onto the bridge.

The guard didn't appear surprised at seeing one of the vans belonging to his gang of thieves cross the mysterious span, and disappear into a dark tunnel that had opened in the once-solid wall. Then, even more incredible—the span broke loose from the far bank, and retracted into the same cavity. Like a sliding warehouse door, the gaping mouth closed, and the sudden eerie silence was punctuated by the splashing of a shower of pebbles dislodged from the ledge.

In awed tones, Andy murmured, "It's a bridge—*a phantom bridge!* That's how the headlights we saw from my bedroom window disappeared. No wonder the police could never find a clue about the missing artwork. They're smuggling it into the cave over a disappearing bridge."

As their boat again began moving down river toward the bend, Dave voiced his own thoughts. "You're right. Once inside, they prepare the artwork for shipment, or forge copies for resale." He glanced across to the guard. "You must smuggle the stuff down river in these boats. But to where, and how far could you   go without being caught?"

"You played square with me so I'll do the same for you—although I can't believe I'm doing this," said the man. "There's a private airport about six miles from here. The boats put into an inlet bordering one side of the field, and the cargo is transferred to business jets after dark. The stuff is flown across the Gulf to Mexico, loaded on a freighter, and shipped to South America for sale or transfer to ships going to Europe or Asia. The organization is huge, and many of the local authorities are in the pockets of the gang. There's no way to bust them. They're   clever people."

Dave studied the man's face. "Why *are* you telling us all of this? You know we'll have to let the police know what we've learned."

The man shrugged. "Guess that's why I did it. The sooner the gang is caught, the safer I'll be. My life won't be worth a cent if they catch me now. Besides, if I have to turn state's evidence, it'll go easier on me, won't it?"

126

Dave was slowing as he approached the beach. "That's not up to us, but knowing how badly Lieutenant Parker and the rest of the authorities want to put an end to the thefts, I'd bet they'd work with you if we ask them to."

The crescent of beach glowed white in the moonlight as the prow of the boat scrunched softly up on the sand. The guard glanced first at Dave and then at Andy. "Guess this is my stop. You kids are okay in my book, but you're in more danger than you can imagine from Blake and the Priest. Get outta here as fast as you can.

About three miles down stream, you'll find a canoeing camp. You can get a phone at the dining hall. Now go, before it's too late." The man jumped into the shallow water and sprinted up the beach into the covering growth. He knew that a two-lane road leading to the main highway was nearby, where he was sure to get a ride from a passing trucker.

Dave pulled the shift lever to reverse and lightly tapped the accelerator. Their boat's rumbling idle was abruptly drowned out by the angry roar of an engine behind them. Their kidnappers, after freeing one of the boats, had quietly followed, waiting for the Carvers' to land. A blinding halogen beam impaled them from mid-river as two high-powered rifle bullets skipped off the water on either side.

"Shut it down, kids, or we'll do it for you," came a voice over a bull horn.

With a feeling of resignation bordering on despair, Dave lifted his foot and turned the ignition key to the off position and the throaty rumble of the inboard sighed to a stop. It wasn't hard to place the voice from the dark. Blake had them again, and so did the Priest.

CHAPTER XII
Night Flight

Andy and Dave sat in gloomy silence on the speedboat's rear bench as they returned to the cave. One of the men had taken over the wheel, and Blake sat side-saddle in the front passenger seat, covering them with a no-nonsense machine pistol. His menacing frown made it clear that he was in a dangerous mood.

"You stupid kids have made life rough for me these last few days. It's gonna to be a real pleasure to see you out of it."

"I don't suppose that means you're going to let us go free, does it?" ventured Andy with false bravado. The slight quiver in his voice betrayed his true feelings.

Blake's humorless laugh was the answer that both Carvers expected.

"We're going to give you boys a free flying lesson. Yes, indeed. An exciting flying lesson that you'll remember for all the rest of your lives."

Nothing more was said while they cruised back upriver into the hidden entrance and tied up again at the dock. Blake, the first one out, pointed with his gun barrel towards the elevator. The boys climbed onto the dock and were pushed along by the men who had disembarked from the second boat. Blake entered, punched an elevator button, and the car rattled noisily upwards.

The ride up ended with a jolt and a bounce. The doors opened onto the same level from which they had recently escaped. Andy looked up the office stairs to see the Priest leaning on the rail and studying him. A gun jabbed him in the back, causing him to almost stumble into a four-wheeler.

Dave, furious at seeing his younger cousin threatened, kicked sideways, striking Blake on the wrist. The machine pistol flew from his hand and clattered metallically across the floor, skittering out of arm's reach well under a heavy bench. Growling with pent-up anger, Blake swung at Dave's head. His fist glanced off the young man's temple, sending a shower of brilliant sparks through Dave's mind. As his consciousness faded, he slumped to the floor, vaguely aware of a boot arcing toward his ribs.

The cave was filled with a deafening concussion that echoed back and forth across the vaulted room and in and out of passageways. Blake groaned and fell to the floor, grasping his foot. Blood oozed from the end of his bullet torn boot.

"You've shot me, you crazy..."

A second bullet slammed into the cave floor next to him and ricocheted off into a side tunnel. Pieces of razor-edged shale peppered Blake's exposed hands and face. The man moaned in pain and fear.

"I warned you to keep your hands off those boys," came the chilling voice from the landing. "Apparently, you have some trouble understanding me. I trust the rest of you men aren't cursed with the same ignorance."

The outlaws silently glanced at each other and then back up to the Priest. Not surprisingly, there were no others who indicated a need for further instruction.

"Cowboy, see that Blake is tended to. Then get up here for my orders."

Dave felt like retching; his head throbbed like a jungle drum. Andy wiped his cousin's face with a rag soaked in water from a glass on their meal tray. The bruise left Dave's temple swollen and discolored. Andy worried that he may have suffered a concussion.

Dave had a violent fit of coughing that doubled him up and the pressure made his eyes feel like popping out of their sockets. "Let me up...I'm okay. I said..." he bent over in a fit of coughing. "I'm—No...I'm not okay at all." He struggled to control the gagging sensation that washed over him. "Oww, my head. Who hit me? Where are we now?"

Andy dabbed the cool rag on Dave's face again. "We're back in the vault. Blake slugged you again, this time with his fist, and the Priest shot him."

Dave struggled to sit up, and then pressed the heels of both hands against his eyes to relieve the pressure. "Shot him? Is he dead?"

131

"No, but he might be missing a toe or two. He was taken somewhere to have his wound treated. After that, the priest ordered Cowboy to come back and take care of us—whatever that means."

As if on cue, the door swooshed open, and Cowboy stepped into the vault and strode over to Dave. "You well enough to walk?" he asked. "Or do I have to get someone to carry you?"

In answer, Dave leaned on Andy arm, and pushed himself up onto his feet. Another wave of nausea sweep over him, but he controlled it. These cold-blooded thieves would get no satisfaction from his injury.

Minutes later, they stood back in the office in front of the Priest, who glared at them. "What happened to the second guard who helped you to escape?"

Andy's tone was indignant. "We didn't need anyone to help us escape. The simple truth of the matter is, that we two helpless young teenagers managed to overpower your big tough crooks, take one a prisoner, steal your boat, and get out all by ourselves. As for the guard, he got away from us, but we didn't need him anymore."

The Priest slammed his open hand on the desk, jarring a cup filled with pens to the floor. "Well, those same two teenagers are right back in front of me, and they are about to wish they had minded their own business and let mine alone."

"*YOUR BUSINESS?!*" roared Dave, the effort jolting his still aching head and eyes. "You call it *your business* to steal people's hard-earned art collections and sell it to other criminals? You're nothing but thieving low-life crooks whose free days are numbered. The police know where we are, and they'll be here soon."

The Priest was not amused. "I heard your amateur attempt to convince us of that story through the security system. I have sources to keep me informed of everything that goes on in the Sheriff's department. They haven't a clue, and by the time they do—we'll be long gone." He paused for effect. "And so will you."

He turned to Cowboy who had been watching with grudging admiration when Dave faced up to the volatile leader.

"Take them to the plane," the Priest snapped. "It should already be loaded. You know what has to be done. See that you do it right, or I'll add some of *your* toes to my trophy collection. Now get out of here!"

Cowboy's jaw tightened as he pointed at the door with his western style six-shot revolver, and shepherded his prisoners back to the boat dock.

They had returned to the river, traveling by boat for almost an hour when the third man with them tugged on Cowboy's sleeve and pointed to a ledge fifty feet above the river. A flashlight blinked twice, three times, and twice again. The boat pilot answered with two blinks from his own penlight and then switched on the boat's brilliant spotlight. It swept the shoreline, stopping on a large tree which overhung the bank. Idling carefully toward the drooping branches, the boat passed through them. The mouth of a small tributary was hidden by the natural camouflage afforded by the foliage. The boat, with three men and their captives, made its slow way up the narrow and meandering waterway. Ten minutes later they were approaching a relatively new dock that had appeared in the brilliant circle of their light. They tied up alongside, and all five climbed out to be confronted by a trio of heavily armed men. There's no honor among thieves, but there's also not much trust, thought Andy.

"This way," growled a burly man in filthy jeans and shirt. "My guys're almost done loading the stuff on the plane. Who's flyin'?"

"I am," declared Cowboy. "I'm also going to teach these boys to fly." His companions from the boat laughed. The Carvers did not.

Filthy Jeans spoke. "You people are crazy. I'll be glad when we finish this business and go our separate ways. There's only four hours left before dawn starts breaking. Let's get going." He turned on his heel and disappeared into the almost invisible path cut into the head-high brush. Soon they were climbing up a tree-covered hill to an unseen destination.

The twin-engine Lear 25 jet, equipped with extended-range wing tanks, was positioned on the runway of a private airport. The cargo and passenger doors were open.

The soft whine of the port engine at idle reached the cousins' ears as they broke out of the surrounding woods.

"I can't tell the color or logo in this light," whispered Dave, "but I'll bet that's the same small jet that nearly collided with my airliner that I flew in on. I hope Cowboy isn't the same jock that flew it that day."

The Carvers had to duck their heads in order to board the low-ceilinged aircraft, then were nudged down the aisle into facing seats at the left rear of the passenger compartment. Cowboy produced two pair of handcuffs and secured their wrists to the armrests. They could hear muffled banging as a dozen containers from the boat were loaded into the baggage compartments in the belly and rear of the plane.

Cowboy was obviously in pain from the growing infection in his leg as took his seat in the cockpit. He was quickly joined by another man whom neither Carver had seen before. Dave concluded from the earlier conversation between Cowboy and the men standing on the runway, that the Priest was commandeering airplanes from other shady operations. The copilot must belong to one of those. The second man retracted the stairs and locked the clam-shell cabin door before making his way forward.

For fifteen minutes, the cousins could hear the two speaking in low tones as they programmed the flight computer and went over the checklist. The starboard engine began to spool up and then added its own distinct whine to its already idling mate.

Minutes later the jet taxied to the end of the runway. After short pause to complete the takeoff checklist, there was a ground-shaking roar as the powerful Lear ate up the mile-long runway and rocketed into a starless night—a night that wrapped its blackness around Dave and Andy's future—whatever that might turn out to be.

The cousins had been right about one thing, Lt. Parker, after being pulled from a meeting when the boys hadn't returned by dinner by the near frantic call from Andy's mother, had dispatched a helicopter and a squad of officers to the Gorge.

They had discovered the ATV tracks from the day before, but no trace of any new ones. There was no further reason to believe that Dave and Andy had returned to the mountainside, so the search for them was then centered around Stockbridge.

Martin tried unsuccessfully to assure Karen that the boys were okay. She remembered the detective's warning that the gang involved in the robberies would not hesitate to harm anyone who interfered with their criminal activities.

As darkness fell over Stockbridge, Martin's brave front began to show signs of cracking. He called Dave's parents and gave them what few details he knew, and promised to let them know the moment the police located their son.

John and Katie had experienced their share of anxious moments during the times that Dave had been involved in adventures with hidden dangers. If their son and Andy were not back by noon the next day, they promised Martin and Karen they would arrive in Colorado on the earliest flight available.

In his downtown office, Lt. Parker finished off his third cup of vending machine coffee in less than an hour. He angrily crumpled the empty Styrofoam cup and flung it into the wire wastebasket. His rage was aimed at himself for letting those kids get involved.

There was no evidence of foul play in their disappearance, but his gut-feeling told him that they had run afoul of the stolen art ring. Why had he given in? One more black mark for the Mayor to hold against him. Whatever the consequence, he vowed that nothing would stand in the way of his find the Carvers, and of bringing art thieves to justice.

Three hours later there was enough daylight to see their surroundings from the jet's windows. Far below, the Gulf of Mexico was painted with a golden neon path that flowed from the rising sun in the East. The underside of the clouds above the aircraft reflected the purple and reds of the awakening sky. Under other circumstances, the young captives would have given all of their savings for a moment like this.

Neither had ever experienced the power and luxury of flying in a private jet aircraft. Dave struggled to make sense out their being aboard. Why would this gang take him and Andy out of the country which would be adding international kidnapping to their list of crimes.

Andy was facing forward and could see the sunrise beginning to show over the horizon. "Dave! Look, the sun is coming up over our wing at about ten o'clock. We're headed southeast over the Gulf past your home. That could mean we're going to Mexico."

"Maybe," agreed his cousin," but I think that would be more to the south. I'm afraid that unless they make a turn somewhere up ahead, we may end up in Venezuela or even in Columbia."

Andy was dumbstruck. "South America? You're not serious. How could we ever make it back home from there? We don't speak the language and our passports are back home."

"Calm down, first things first. Let's find out where we're going before we jump to any conclusions. I'm reasonably sure that they don't mean to harm us. All that talk was to scare us into keeping quiet."

"Do you really believe that?" asked Andy as he studied Dave's eyes.

The older Carver hesitated before softly answering. "No—but I don't want to think about the alternatives."

CHAPTER XIII
Welcome Company

Even though their movement was limited by the handcuffs locked to the armrests, the boys were able to easily see out of windows on both sides of the narrow business jet. They had been airborne almost four hours, and there was no sight of land in any direction.

"We must be almost over the middle of the Gulf by now," speculated Andy.

Dave nodded and leaned out to see what was going on in the cockpit. The door was propped open so that Cowboy could keep an eye on them. The two men were talking in low tones and studying a navigation chart. In mid-sentence, Cowboy glanced back at the Carvers, then turned back and spoke into his radio mike.

"Wonder what that crack about teaching us to fly meant?" wondered Andy aloud. "It's a little difficult flying a jet from back here in the cabin even without these bracelets." He rattled the cuffs against his armrests to make the point. "Besides, how would they have known we were interested in being pilots? Everyone back home knows how much we want to build and fly our own plane, but we never mentioned that to any of this crooked bunch."

Dave turned to study his cousin's face. "I've been thinking about that, and I'm afraid that's not what they meant."

Andy was puzzled. "What are you saying?"

"Remember they mentioned something about dumping us in the Gulf? I don't think they were talking about a ship—I think they mean to dump us from this plane!"

Horrified at the thought, Andy's mouth gaped open and closed like a fish out of water. He swallowed hard and stared down at the water thousands of feet below the wing. "They wouldn't dare," he whispered hoarsely shaking his head in disbelief. "They wouldn't dare. Besides, you can't just open the door on a jet. Everything would be blown out, including those murderous thugs."

"Shut up, you two," warned Cowboy from up front. "Sorry I can't offer you any coffee, tea or milk. Anyhow, it'd just be a waste of good food." The copilot snickered.

Dave lightly knocked his knee against Andy's and nodded his head toward the nearest window. The younger Carver stared straight out, and then glanced back toward the tail. Sunlight glinted off a shiny object several miles behind them and to the east. They watched as it drew closer and closer. Finally, they recognized it as a Cessna Citation jet similar in size to the one that they were on. The men piloting their Lear had apparently not spotted it as yet. At least they hadn't made any evasive moves to lose it in the clouds. Dave's first thought was that it might be another member of the same gang making a delivery run.

As it slowly approached, the boys could make out the tail number. Now they could tell that it was a government aircraft from the department of Alcohol, Tobacco and Firearms, probably hunting for drug smugglers. The Cessna stayed back and remained at an angle that made it impossible to be seen by Cowboy and his copilot from the cockpit.

Cowboy's voice interrupted them. "Glad to see you boys enjoyin' the view. Remember how in grade school you studied about when it was time for baby birds to learn to use their wings, their parents pushed them out of the nests? It was 'Fly or Die' time. In a few more miles, we'll begin *your* flying lessons using the same method." The laughter that followed sent waves of fear and nausea through the Carver cousins.

Sweat dribbled from Andy's forehead into his eyes, and he wiped the sleeve on his free arm across them. "If only we had some way of signaling the ATF guys in the other jet," he whispered. He checked out the window and noticed that the plane had dropped back at least a half mile or more. "Maybe we ought to tell Cowboy that we're being followed. He wouldn't dare do anything to us if he's being watched."

Dave's face reflected his feeling of hopelessness. "No good. They're too far back now, and these guys would just give them the slip. I'm afraid the Feds are getting ready to turn back. We should have done something to attract their attention when they were alongside…"

On a sudden inspiration, Dave reached into his left jacket pocket and pulled out the chrome gas cap he had found back at Killigan's Gorge. He polished the mud splotched surface on his sleeve and held it up to the window. Andy watched with growing curiosity and then realized that his cousin was using it as a signaling mirror. The sun caught the shiny surface and sent brilliant flashes of light back toward the AFT jet.

The agent in the copilot seat was the first to notice the reflections, and pointed out the flashing signal to his partner. They edged back closer to the source.

Andy caught Dave's attention and silently mouthed "YES!" as he saw them approaching. His cousin began to methodically flash $S-O-S$ to the Cessna.

Cowboy had left his seat, and was pulling his gun from his jacket pocket, when he saw the boys leaning against the window and noticed the flashes of light reflecting on the window frame. Even a schoolboy can recognize the regularity of a distress signal. He crouched to peer out the nearest window, and was startled to see an airplane flying in formation with them.

"Get away from there," he growled, grabbing Dave's arm, sending the gas cap bouncing off the lavatory door. The angry pilot backhanded him across the same temple that had been bruised by Blake back at the cave. Dave groaned and sank back into his seat.

142

"You are all nothing but a bunch of lousy cowards!" shouted Andy. "You haven't got the guts to face anyone on equal terms. You hide behind your van or gun and need to have someone tied up to prove you're some kind of tough guy. You're nothing but a yellow…"

"Shut up!" shouted Cowboy, slapping Andy across the mouth. "Those guys can't help you. They're way out of their territory. I promise you this—as soon as they turn back, you and your trouble-makin' cousin are gonna set the record for the world's highest swan dive."

Andy's voice was filled with defiance, now that he felt he had nothing else to lose. "I happen to know that you can't open the door on this jet without blowing everything out, including yourself."

"Wrong. We can slow this bird to one hundred thirty knots before it stalls. Once we're below five-thousand feet, the cabin can be depressurized. All I have to do is override the safety switches, open the door, and, 'Bye, Bye, Birdies'. Oh, and please be careful not to get sucked into the engine. You wouldn't want to be the cause of us flaming out this far from shore."

His sarcasm was halted as the ATF jet drew parallel to their windows. They were close enough to clearly see the face of the pilot agent staring at them.

"Hey," came a shout from their own cockpit. "There's a plane off our left wing."

"I know that, you idiot." snapped Cowboy. "They're Feds. Can we lose them?"

"Not a chance. The cloud cover's too thin. That Citation can keep up with our Lear Jet. Maybe they'll have to turn back soon since they can't land and refuel where we're going....Wait, they're radioing on the clear channel."

As Cowboy and Andy turned toward the open cockpit door to hear the message coming from the ATF plane, Dave groaned and began to stir.

"Oh, my head. It's going to explode. I don't think I can take much more of this, Andy. Where are we?"

"Stay quiet, Dave. Cowboy slugged you again. Those AFT guys are just off the wing."

Dave, with great effort, pulled himself up to the window. He could see the pilot studying his face. Dave turned his body to block Cowboy's view and raised his hand, forming his fingers into the shape of a pistol pointed at his own head. The agent nodded, understanding that Dave was a prisoner.

"Get away from that window," snarled Cowboy, jerking Dave backward into the seat. "What are they saying on the radio?" he shouted to the other man.

"They want to know our destination and cargo," came the answer.

"Don't say a word. Just start climbing slowly to forty thousand and see if they follow."

Andy breathed a sigh of relief. Thanks to his cousin's ingenuity in using the gas cap, they were at least saved from taking that fatal plunge into the gulf—for now. Questions remained. Would the AFT plane be able to dog them all the way to their landing? What would happen if they did? What if they didn't? What other threats would face them once they were on the ground, and where would *on the ground* be?

Two more hours passed. Both aircraft remained in formation as they flew high above the scattered clouds. The ATF jet was equipped with long range tanks and seemed in no hurry to turn back.

"Looks like they plan to follow us all the way in," observed Cowboy. "Try to raise camp and arrange for an unwelcoming party to discourage them. I'm taking us down to the deck for the final approach."

Dave leaned over to Andy. "Five hours of flying was not enough time to reach South America. At about four hundred miles per hour, we must be about two thousand miles southeast of Stockbridge. That would put us somewhere near Mexico or Central America—maybe Guatemala or Honduras."

Andy shook his head at his cousin's grasp of geography. Now he wished that his own studies in that field had been better. He returned his gaze to the window, watching as they lost altitude and speed, happy to see the agents staying right with them.

Unexpectedly, a commuter-sized turboprop aircraft roared over top of the ATF jet and rocked it violently with its prop wash. Only five thousand feet above the water, the Feds wrestled desperately with their bucking aircraft. It was a haunting replay for Dave as he experienced, for the second time since coming to his cousin's home, an aircraft fighting for its life.

With less than five hundred feet to spare, the agents brought the Cessna under control and banked away from the returning bandit. With a top speed of around three-hundred knots, the turbo prop would not be able to catch the fleeing jet, nor did it try. The pilot's interest seemed only to be in chasing the Feds away from their hidden airfield.

"Will they come back?" whispered Andy?

Dave sadly shook his head and replied. "I doubt it. They must be close to their one-way fuel limit and another brush with that turboprop could be fatal. I have an idea that they've already reported our tail number and description. Maybe the local police will send out a plane."

"At least Cowboy and that other creep don't know any more about what could happen than we do," said Andy. "That should make them think twice before they try to dump us out."

"I'm not gonna' warn you guys again to shut up," shouted Cowboy. "You think you're so smart with that gas cap trick, but it only bought you a little more time. There's more than one way to skin a cat—especially where we're headed."

Andy fell back against the seat his face a mask of resignation. Dave felt responsible for his younger cousin and tried to put on a more positive expression. It wasn't working all that well.

Andy was the first to spot the break in the unchanging line of the water below. The horizon took on the uneven look of land. He inclined his head toward the window as a signal to Dave, who then leaned forward to study their rapidly approaching destination. As they drew nearer, the boys could see that there was nothing but thick jungle and low hills—no signs of civilization anywhere.

Fifteen minutes passed before the sound of gear and flap motors announced that they were on final approach. Far from being out of danger, the Carvers knew that their brush with death was only a delay, but at least it gave them yet another chance to escape—if only they knew from where—and how it could be done!

CHAPTER XIV
Where Are We?

The boys could still see ocean beneath them as the sleek jet dropped below the thousand foot level. At five hundred feet, they were soaring over jungle growth that seemed impenetrable. Trees on each side of the Lear loomed higher than the jet as it skimmed over tangled undergrowth. When it seemed that they were about to impact with the deadly green carpet, the near end of a packed dirt strip flashed beneath the wheels. The set down was bumpy, but the Carvers grudgingly admired Cowboy's landing on this less than commercial quality runway.

The engines were still spooling down when the copilot opened the outside door and then freed the boys from their handcuffs. He produced a handgun and nodded toward the stairs. Emerging from the relatively dark interior of the Lear, Dave and Andy blinked back the burning brightness of the near-equatorial sun. Around the cleared strip, they could make out a number of low buildings hidden under the trees, and a taller one, probably a hanger, draped with camouflage netting.

"Welcome to our little Paradise, kids," said Cowboy as he joined them. "Sorry you missed your chance to earn your wings, but there's always another day—or another way. Anyhow, I'm going to give you a tour of what you've wanted to see from the beginning. Everything outside of this cozy little community is snakes, quicksand bogs, jungle rot, and hungry carnivores. We're quite proud of our little home away from home. It's unfortunate, but you won't be permitted to send your folks any postcards from here."

Dave was watching men unloading boxes from the baggage compartment of the jet. Since only small objects could be carried, it was obvious that the turbo props were used for most of the cargo carrying tasks. The Lear was used to carry passengers, minor art objects, and, no doubt, money from black-market sales.

A short, stocky man dressed in a dusty, sweat-stained, white suit and discolored Panama hat ambled toward them, mopping his brow with a handkerchief. "Ah, we have company. These are, undoubtedly, the two young gentlemen our priestly friend told me about. I've done a little checking up on them; they have a reputation for, shall we say, amateur snooping. My name is Señor Alvaronz, unofficial Mayor of our little jungle town." He doffed his hat and made an exaggerated bow.

"Where are we?" demanded Andy.

"Patience, my young amigo. Where you are is of no importance. Where you are going will be more interesting. But for now, let our friend show you around." He nodded at Cowboy and turned toward the hanger, his shoes raising small puffs of dry dust as he strode away.

"Señor Alvaronz is our shipping coordinator for South America," explained Cowboy, exhibiting pride in comparing his criminal operation with a legitimate business. "The real and duplicated artwork comes here by plane, is packaged for shipping and loaded aboard tramp steamers for delivery to Venezuela and Guyana. From there, it is sent to buyers around the world or sold at secret auctions. The big building is where we hanger and service the planes, and those huts over there are barracks for the men who work here."

Dave, interested in spite of the danger to him and Andy, could not resist asking questions as long as Cowboy seemed content to answer him. "Are all those men part of your gang?"

"We prefer to call ourselves a company. After all, we run everything like one."

Andy snorted. "If you guys are so good at acting like a legitimate business, why didn't you start one instead of stealing from innocent people? You wouldn't have to jump at your own shadow, and you wouldn't have to hang around in pest-holes like in this jungle."

Cowboy's reply was matter-of-fact. "Maybe so, but there's a lot more excitement and money to be had in our line of work." He suddenly lost any trace of humor. "Enough preaching. Your cousin—Dave, isn't it?—wanted to know who all these men were. Most are prisoners that we freed when we broke Señor Alvaronz out of jail. They couldn't stay around the cities to risk being caught again, and besides, they owed us something for getting them out."

"It sort of takes the profit out of the 'business' when you have this many people on the payroll," remarked Dave.

"They get fed, housed, and protected. They won't get paid off 'til we're ready to close down. Each man will get what's coming to him at that time."

Andy shuddered. "I can imagine what that will be."

Cowboy pointed to a large Quonset hut set back under the trees. "Over there," he ordered.

Dave cautiously pushed open the door. The lack of air conditioning was overwhelmingly apparent as the hot damp air struck them when they stepped inside. There was also a sickening mix of odors; leftover food, overripe fruit, and sweaty clothes.

"Phew," gasped Dave. "How can you stand to have to be in here?"

"Simple. I don't have to. Whenever I'm down here, I sleep in the hanger. That's where the only air conditioner is installed. We have to keep it cool for the electronics we use to service the planes. Now, have a seat until Alvaronz comes back. You're gonna be his problem after today."

Cowboy produced the pair of familiar handcuffs again, and secured the boys to a large conduit attached to the fuse box on one wall. "Promise me you'll stay right there until he gets here."

His smirk angered Andy, who aimed a kick in his direction. Cowboy side-stepped out of range, but the sudden move made him wince from the pain in his swollen leg. The infection was beginning to tell on him, and sweat ran in rivulets down his face. He backed toward the door and disappeared outside, closing them inside with the heat and the smells.

"Cowboy seems really sick and appears to be limping more each time we see him. Wonder what's wrong with his leg? Do you think it's from that first karate kick you gave him?" asked Andy, struggling with the handcuffs.

"I doubt it, but there's something bothering him. That might be to our advantage. In the meantime, don't mess up your wrists trying to get out of these cuffs," advised Dave. "Let's spend the time comparing notes to see how we can escape this mess. I saw several trucks, but the jungle is too thick to drive anywhere outside the camp.

"You heard the Cowboy's description about the snakes, quicksand, and all the things that go bump in the night. That rules out going by foot. Neither of us could fly the planes that we've seen, so that eliminates three methods of escape."

Andy nodded. "We flew in over water that was not too far away. Maybe we could find a boat."

"Maybe so," agreed Dave as he tested his handcuffs for looseness. "The problem is, we don't know where we are or where we could go if we did have a boat. We might be hundreds of miles from any civilization. Anything would be better than this, though."

"Dave," exclaimed Andy with a touch of excitement. I have an idea. Do you still have the SkyTraker software disk I gave you?"

His cousin patted his jacket over the inside pocket. "Yeah, it's right here still in the plastic cover, why?"

"Look over on the desk. There's a computer. If we can get a peek at the night sky and locate a couple of major stars or planets, and if we can get into one of the computers to load the program, and if we can get hold of a compass and a protractor and level..."

"Wait a minute. All the 'ifs' aside, are you saying we can really find out where we are?"

"I'm saying that we can at least know the latitude and longitude of this camp. That would help us once we find a navigational chart like the ones they keep in airplanes or maybe somewhere in the hanger."

Dave began to feel his cousin's excitement. "There's a couple more 'if's' I'm afraid," he said with a sad smile. "*If* we can get loose when the stars are out, and *if* we can then get back to this computer before they move us out of here or—or worse."

The door opened suddenly. Señor Alvaronz, followed by Cowboy, stepped inside, brushing the dust off his pants with his Panama. "Madre de Dios, it's hot! Ah, my young amigos, are you enjoying your visit? No, no, it's not necessary to thank me for my hospitality. But wait, no one has offered you anything to eat or drink? Where are your manners, Señor Ritter?"

The Carvers looked at each other. That was the first time anyone had attached a name to the one called Cowboy. His whole outfit and six-gun thing must be a spin-off from having the last name of the famous cowboy actor.

"Let me guess," blurted out Andy. "Your friends, if you have any, call you Tex."

Cowboy spun around in anger. "Shut your smart-alecky mouth, kid. For your information, I have a ton of friends, and yes—they call me Tex. Since you're not one of those friends, you don't call me anything."

Cowboy turned back to Alvaronz. "Go ahead and give them food and water if you want, but you know it's just a waste of good supplies. I'll be back to take them to the shed in about twenty minutes." With that, he was gone with an even more noticeable limp.

"Well, amigos, what can I get for you? Ah…how about sandwiches and some bottled water?" He started for the door, picked up a plate from the table, and paused in the doorway. "Si, that will be good. Sorry I have to leave you fastened to that pipe until I return, but I'm sure you understand, no?"

"No!" echoed Andy, with a totally different meaning.

Alvaronz shrugged and closed the door behind him.

Dave had been studying the computer screen during the exchanges between Andy and their captors. "Alvaronz bumped the keyboard when he picked up the plate and caused the screen saver to turn off. Unless my eyes deceive me, that database booted up on the screen could be either a list of their customers or other members of the gang. See, the left column has names, right next to another that might be phone numbers or e-mail addresses.

"The other columns could be codes that stand for what was being delivered or where it came from or something like that. It also looks like dollar amounts listed under the dates at the top. If that's what it is, we should try to use one of their disks to copy the file. Interpol could locate those illegal buyers and maybe even recover much of the stolen art."

"Interpol?" questioned Andy.

"It's an International police system with connections all over the world."

"You think we can get my dad's things back for him? Boy, that would be great. All we have to do is make all of the 'ifs' happen that we talked about."

Dave's stomach rumbled. "I hope he hurries back with some decent food. We haven't eaten since we were back in the cave. Cowboy is serious about not wanting to waste food on us. There's no question that they plan to get kill us and get rid of our bodies."

"Dave! Don't talk that way!" exclaimed Andy.

"Look, cuz, let's not fool ourselves into thinking they'll set us free. We've seen too much, and they have no intentions of letting us tell about it. That's why it's so important that we get our act together and make our plans now."

He was interrupted by the return of Alvaronz, bearing a tray of sandwiches, fruit, and frosted bottles of water. "I'm going to release you one at a time and refasten your handcuffs to these chairs so you can sit at the table and eat. Please don't make me sorry I'm giving you this privilege."

Setting the tray on the table, he moved first Andy and then Dave to the chairs, and then sat opposite them to watch them eat. It was obvious that both boys were extremely hungry, and he felt angry that Cowboy had treated them with such contempt.

"I don't know what you've done to make Señor Ritter mad at you, but I wouldn't keep tempting him. He has a mean streak in him a mile wide."

"What do you intend to do with us?" asked Dave, his mouth stuffed with the meat-filled sandwich.

"You will be put aboard one of our ships and taken to Venezuela. There, in time, you will be turned loose to make your way back home. How do you like the sandwiches?"

"Good," said Andy. "I was so hungry that I could've eaten almost anything"

"I'm glad to hear you say that," said Alvaronz with a broad smile. "Most people from outside the country would rather starve than eat Anaconda."

"Anaconda!" gulped Dave. "You mean like the big snake?"

"Sure. It's pretty good, don't you think? Myself, I like it much better than those giant cockroaches the locals eat."

He shuddered. "But maybe that's a taste you have to acquire."

Dave and Andy fought to keep their stomachs calm. The meat was not all that bad if you forgot where it came from, and they did have to eat something to keep up their strength. Nevertheless, there was no truth in the rumor that snake tasted just like chicken.

"I'll leave you at the table until Señor Ritter comes back. You can't go anywhere dragging those chairs hooked to your wrists. Relax and finish your food and water."

"Wait," said Dave. "How soon does the ship leave?"

"It's almost loaded now, and will sail tomorrow at sunset. We prefer that it be a good distance from our secret little community before someone spots it at sea. I must go and help prepare for their departure. Adios, amigos. We may not meet again."

Dave thumped his palm against the table. "Let's cut out the amigo nonsense, Alvaronz. You know as well as we that this bunch of cutthroats has no intention of setting us free. If we hadn't been followed by a plane full of ATF agents, we'd be fish food at the bottom of the Gulf. You don't seem like the killer type, Señor, why don't you set us free?"

Alvaronz seemed taken back by Dave's outburst. "You are mistaken. I've been with the company since the beginning and have known Cowboy the whole time. He is not the kind to do what you have suggested. What you may have experienced was his way to keep you under control."

Andy leaned forward. "I feel sorry for you, *amigo*," he said with a touch of sarcasm. "You better watch your back when this is over. This so-called company has no intention of paying all of you off, at least in the way you are expecting."

Alvaronz brow knitted in a frown, then relaxed. "As I said, adios, amigos, in case I don't see you again." His parting words rang ominously off the metal walls.

"Oh," groaned Andy when the door was shut. "What can be worse than eating snakes and cockroaches?"

"I tell you what's worse," said Dave grimly. "Their ship sails in less than thirty hours, and that's all the time we have to work out our escape plan. If we fail, we could be lost in South America for years, or end up on the bottom of the Atlantic."

CHAPTER XV
SkyTraker

Dave hoped that Andy would be able to handle everything that was to fall on his shoulders over the next few hours. Most of the success of their plan depended on his younger cousin. They had been missing from Stockbridge for more than a day. Uncle Martin and Aunt Karen must be getting frantic by now. Would Lieutenant Parker have sent a search party to the mountains? Would they find the four-wheeler tracks near the church?

The door slammed open against the wall. Cowboy stormed into the hut, throwing a stack of charts onto the desk. "Stupid, stupid, stupid! Everyone in this cesspool is a stupid idiot. What're you starin' at?" he barked at Andy.

"Just wondered why you're so worked up here in Paradise."

Cowboy made a move toward Andy with an upraised hand, but Dave averted the attack by an unexpected remark.

"Listen, Mr. Ritter. How about laying off the rough stuff? We may not be on the same side, but I wanted to tell you how much Andy and I admired your handling of the Lear on the dirt runway out there."

159

The comment took the man completely by surprise. His hand dropped to his side as he turned toward Dave. "Yeah? What makes you kids *think* you know anything about flying?"

"Andy and I have been working on plans to build our own plane. We've studied a lot about flying have both soloed. We also travel a lot by air and know a good pilot when we meet one."

"Well, it won't do you any good to try to flatter me with any of your amateur compliments, but thanks anyway. These morons I work with don't appreciate what goes on outside of their little corner of the world. If things were different, I'd show you two a real homebuilt plane, one I'm working on—but thing aren't different, and that's that.

"Yeah," said Dave, gritting his teeth, "that's that. So why are you so upset?"

Cowboy snorted and limped over to pick up one of the charts that had fallen off the table. "It's those so-called mechanics that our *Señor* Alvaronz has working for him. They contaminated the fuel in my Lear by accidentally pumping cleaning fluid into my tanks. They had the stuff stored in an old fuel drum without changing the label. Instead of getting out of here this evening, I've got to flush out the tanks and the whole fuel system. If that wasn't bad enough, my copilot got himself too drunk to fly, and that means I'll have to go it alone."

Andy got in the spirit of keeping Cowboy's mind off slapping them around. "That makes you pretty lucky that you found out about the cleaning fluid before taking off. Are sure it was a mistake? Maybe these guys don't like you any more than we do."

"Think you're funny, kid? We'll see how much you're laughing a few hours from now."

He crossed to the table and unlocked their handcuffs. Then he ordered Dave and Andy to link arms before fastening them again. The boys had to move crablike to follow him to the door.

"Makes it a little awkward to run away, don't you think?" He pointed across the clearing to a smaller building. "The shed is good and solid so I'll turn you loose in there to eat and sleep tonight. Tomorrow you get to go on a cruise. Nothing like the smell of a sea breeze to clear one's head." Cowboy herded the cousins through the door and prodded them to the front of the shed. "Here kid, take this key and open the door. And no tricks, understand? Once you're inside, I'll take off your cuffs for the night."

Andy turned the key in the lock, pushed open the door, and returned the key to Cowboy. He motioned them inside, removed the handcuffs, and strode out, slamming the door. A loud click signaled that the lock tumblers had engaged.

Andy walked around the cramped space taking inventory of the shed's contents. There were two sleeping bags spread out on straw, one chair and a small table, a bottle of water, some type of green fruit, a ceiling fan with a bare light bulb, and a box of automobile or aircraft parts.

The walls and roof were made of corrugated steel and the floor was constructed from heavy wood planking. The shed measured twelve feet on each side and was nearly ten feet tall at the peak of the roof.

Dave had immediately stretched out on one of the sleeping bags and was busy reviewing his plans for escape. Andy nudged him with the water bottle, which he gratefully accepted, gulping down several swallows. The heat was relentless in this metal building. The only light came from a square foot of fiberglass in the roof and two small air vents at the top of each peaked wall. Andy reached for the fan's pull chain. The bulb worked; the fan didn't. No surprise there, he thought.

Dave stood up and crossed to the box of parts. He poured them out on the floor and began to sort through the collection, hoping to find something to use as a tool for escape. He held up a bracket and a filter bowl from a large carburetor.

"We can use this bracket as a pry bar on the floor planks and this bowl to dig under the walls. It'll be hard work, but we can both take turns. We can store the dirt under the straw and cover it with the sleeping bags. There's about six hours of light left, and we need to get over to the office and work on the computer as quickly as it gets dark."

Andy listened intently, then added his own thoughts. "I still think we should see if we can discover a trail to the beach, and find a way to put miles between us and this base."

Dave nodded in agreement. "There might be enough time to check out that possibility and still make it back here if we don't find a boat. We could also explore the idea of stowing away on one of the planes and hijacking it once we're clear of land. If we can come up with a decent weapon, we could force the pilots to fly us back to the States."

"That sounds like an even better idea," said Andy. "How about rigging up a Molotov cocktail?"

"The fire thing almost worked for us back at the church, but I don't think they'd believe we would risk our own lives in an airplane. Right now, our biggest concern is being able to get out of this shed in time."

"That's not a major problem," declared Andy. "You have that crude, but sturdy, crowbar along with that tiny, but useful, bowl for digging—while all I have is this key to open the door." He produced the magic piece of brass with an impishly triumphant smile.

"How did you—you switched keys, didn't you?"

"Well, I admit that I placed my parent's barn door in jeopardy if Ritter ever gets back to Stockbridge. Both keys were a similar type, and I figure he's too concerned about his contaminated fuel to notice any difference or to come back here. Señor Alvaronz probably has his own key, so he won't know anything about this one."

Andy was right. When the guard sent by Alvaronz to bring them more food and water arrived later that evening, he came and left, totally unaware that the prisoners were but a key turn from freedom.

The sounds of the jungle night were unnerving to the two stealthy figures who crept along the border of the camp toward the Quonset hut. They had stuffed their sleeping bags with straw, dumped the remaining food and water containers into an old pillow case they had found, and left, locking the door behind them in case someone decided to check in on the prisoners. Dave pointed to a worn-out army truck parked nearby.

"I'll see if I can find a flashlight in the truck. I have a book of matches that someone left in the hut, but we need something more dependable and long lasting."

"Just be careful," Andy whispered. "The dome light might go on when you open the door."

"Thanks for the warning, but those old military trucks had no lights except the slotted headlights. Not too good to let an enemy know where you were at night, you know."

The side window was open and Dave could see a flashlight clipped to the bottom of the dash. He pulled it free, covered it with his palm, and flipped the switch. His hand glowed a soft pink. He switched the light off and then pocketed an object he spotted hanging on the mirror. Back in the trees, he showed Andy the bonus that he had found...a surveyor's compass.

Over the end of the runway, they spotted two bright planets, which Andy identified as Venus, and, possibly,

Jupiter. He took the compass from Dave, and pointed it toward each of the planets in turn, asking his cousin to help him remember the readings. Then he produced a square of paper from his pocket and folded it diagonally to make a triangle.

"Watch this," he whispered. He took out the water bottle and set it on top of an old fuel drum. Carefully he wedged pieces of bark under the bottom of the barrel until the water was level with one of the rings molded around the container.

"See, when the water is even on all sides, I know that the top of the bottle is level. This folded square produces a forty-five degree angle. If I set this vertically on top of the bottle, then sight along the diagonal toward one of the planets, I can get a close estimate of how many degrees it is above the horizon. It's a rough protractor, but it will put us in the ball park. The compass will show us the direction of each planet."

Andy took his readings, noted the time on his watch, and started toward the hut. "I hope it's not locked," he said, holding up crossed fingers.

Luckily for the boys it wasn't. No one was in the area as they pushed their way into the darkened interior. The only light came from the tiny moving images on the computer screen saver. They moved to the keyboard, and Dave handed Andy the SkyTraker disk. Moments later, his cousin had booted up the program and was entering the data they had collected. A astronomical chart of the planets and constellations appeared and, with great delight, Andy pointed out the two planets on the screen.

"After I entered today's date, time, and the location of these planets, the program was able to calculate the one spot on earth where the sky would appear like this. I'll duck outside and see if I can identify some of the constellations just to be sure."

Seconds later, he returned and made a few minor adjustments. The coordinates located them at 21 degrees, 30 minutes North; 97 degrees, 31 minutes West. Grabbing a pen from the desk, Andy wrote the information on a scrap of paper. He smiled triumphantly as he held up his calculations. "I remember that New Orleans is right at 30 degrees North and 90 degrees West, so I figure we must be about six hundred miles southeast of Louisiana."

Dave patted his cousin on the back. "Since we only came across a short stretch of land, and given the cruising speed of a Lear and our flying time, that would put us somewhere on the Yucatan Peninsula. We're in Mexico, probably not too far from the western tip of Cuba."

"There are a few disks in this drawer," exclaimed Andy. "I'll clear some of them off and see if I can get a copy of the database you saw."

He closed the SkyTraker program and handed it back to Dave, then he erased several floppy disks. Andy called up the file manager and began to copy all the most recently dated files he could fit on the floppies. Dave, in the meantime, had been studying the charts that Cowboy had left behind. He selected one that contained the coordinates that Andy had calculated, and, folding it as small as was possible, tucked it into his inner pocket.

Andy was preparing to load another disk when they heard a hollow metallic boom followed by cursing outside. Someone had apparently run into the barrel that he had set out for his sighting table. Quickly, Andy returned the computer to the database program as he had found it. He hoped the screen saver was set to boot up in a few seconds, since the chart now on the screen would be a dead giveaway that someone had been on the keyboard. He held his breath as he and Dave squeezed behind a stack of cardboard boxes in the corner.

Just as the doorknob began to turn, the screen saver kicked in and the bright light from the monitor dimmed. Cowboy pushed his way into the office and flipped on the overhead light. Spotting his charts, he tucked them under his arm, turned off the light, and slammed the door.

Beads of sweat stung Dave's eyes as he considered how close they had come to being caught. "Let's return to the shed before we plan our next move," he urged.

Three minutes later, they pulled the door to their makeshift prison closed behind them, turned the key, and sank down on the bulging sleeping bags. The older Carver spread out the chart. He cupped the flashlight in his hand so only a sliver of light leaked between his fingers onto the paper. Tracing Andy's coordinates, Dave triumphantly pointed to a spot on the Yucatan Peninsula.

"We were right. Thanks to your program I've located us about twenty miles west of Cancun."

"That's super news, Dave. We'd better not wait too long to head for the beach if we want to find a boat that can get us out of here. It'll be daylight before we know it, and we need all the darkness we can get."

"Right. I just need some time to let my heart slow down. I swear I thought it was about to jump out of my chest. Can you imagine what would have happened if Cowboy had seen us and found the disks and the chart? Well, no matter. I still have the compass and flashlight in my jacket pocket—do you have the food sack?"

"Yes. It's stuffed under my shirt. Let's get going," urged Andy.

A Spanish-accented voice cut through the night outside. "Hey, amigos...wake up!" It was Señor Alvaronz! He and two men were heading across the clearing toward the shed.

Frantically, the cousins emptied the straw from the sleeping bags and dove inside. As the door opened and the room flooded with light, they propped themselves up and began rubbing their eyes.

"What's happening," mumbled Dave in his best imitation of an awakened sleeper.

"You are going—how do you say—bye bye?"

Andy's eyes opened wide as he bolted upright. "What do you mean? I thought the ship was sailing tomorrow night."

Alvaronz shrugged. "Sorry, change of plans. The ship's captain is worried that the Federales may fly back over this area to search for you and he wants to be away before dawn. Get yourselves up. Vamos amigos."

Outside, the Carvers were herded into a battered army Jeep driven by a Mexican dressed in greasy fatigues and a filthy, torn tee-shirt. A second man, a guard, apparently had a matching wardrobe, and carried an ancient rifle

To the boys' surprise, they were not heading north back along the runway to the beach. Instead, their vehicle was driven east on a beaten trail that zigzagged between trees and around oozing swamps. The headlights swept a clear path ahead, and were reflected here and there in the eyes of creatures hiding among the trees and brush. It was all they could do to hang onto the bucking vehicle while it churned through the thick growth which constantly fought to regain its rightful place in the ecology.

Dave was first to notice the thick rope hanging from a tree branch above the trail. He didn't understand the purpose for it being there so far from camp. The end was hanging low enough to strike the windshield, and the driver and guard were involved in an argument that took their attention away from what was ahead.

Only few seconds before the collision, Dave realized that the rope was a huge snake—an anaconda. Andy's eyes widened as he recognized the creature. With a loud thump, the snake's head smashed into the windshield and all one hundred pounds of potential sandwich meat fell into the back seat.

The Jeep swerved, narrowly missing a tree as the captive boys wrestled the dying snake over the side. It was all Andy could do to keep from throwing up as he used his shirttail to wipe the snake's blood and gore from his face and hands.

There was no more time to think about their gruesome encounter, however, for they now heard metallic bumping and banging, and the shouting of men somewhere up ahead. Rounding a long curve, they suddenly burst out into a clearing that blazed with lights mounted on tall poles. In the focus of the beams, an ominous, black, eighteen-thousand ton freighter lay moored in a fair-sized tributary. Its paint was peeling, and rusty water seemed to drip from every opening. The faded name on the bow was *La Estrella Negra*...The Black Star.

CHAPTER XVI
The Black Star

Señor Alvaronz jumped from the jeep with a canvas bag flung across his shoulder and strode quickly to the ship. The boys watched him board before being bullied from their seats by the men from the camp. Two wide gangways bridged up from the dock to *La Estrella Negra*. One led to the cargo doors in the side of the ship's hull, and the other rose at a steeper angle to the main deck.

Food supplies were being loaded by forklift up the aft ramp. The guards jabbed rifle barrels into the Carvers' ribs to force the unwilling passengers up the forward gangway. The ship's crane was lowering water-tight crates into one of the holds. Labels identified the contents as machine parts.

Clever, thought Dave. The stolen artwork is probably concealed beneath false bottoms of those crates. Anyone inspecting them would find nothing but heavy castings or machine parts inside. Even if the inspector were not bribed, no one would want to take the trouble of removing all the contents for a thorough search.

Andy grunted as he slipped on the damp surface of the gangway, nearly falling under the ropes into the rancid black water below.

"Hey—watch it, kid! I guarantee you don't wanna fall in this stinkin' river," warned the guard. "There's some really nasty critters in this water that'll take off a leg or arm before you get totally wet. 'Course, if you *really* like to swim that be arranged after we're well at sea."

The second guard gave the man a warning glance, then ordered Dave and Andy to turn left when they reached the deck. Walking aft, they passed close to the ship's captain and Señor Alvaronz. The latter was describing several small figurines laid out on a hatch cover. The captain picked up two of the items and tucked them into his coat pockets. Alvaronz repacked the remainder and stuffed the bag under his arm. As he turned, he saw the boys, and gestured for the guards to halt.

"Ah, my young amigos. I *do* apologize for the poor meals and lack of sleep. I've instructed the captain to be sure that you are well fed and that you get plenty of rest. Trust me when I say that you will get back to your homes pronto—that is, if you don't make trouble for these people. Si? Buena suerte—good luck." He waved and disappeared down the forward gangway.

Dave and Andy were herded into a small stern cabin. The door clanged shut behind them. Two wall-hung cots with their dirty rumpled blankets and pillows and a single chair leaning drunkenly to one side, took up most of the tiny space. Andy crossed to a porthole and stood on tiptoe to see out as far as possible in each direction.

"Looks like our guards are going back toward the hatch. What's going to happen to us, Dave?"

"Once they get us out to sea, I don't believe they intend to have us set foot on land again. I honestly don't think Señor Alvaronz is aware of any plans to get rid of us. He probably believes they'll turn us loose in Venezuela. If we're to get out of this alive, we have to escape off this ship before it sails."

Andy swallowed painfully. "I'm sure you're right, but I have no idea how we go about it. It sounds like they plan to sail right after sunset. That doesn't give us much time. By the way, did you notice Alvaronz gave the captain several small pieces of artwork?"

"Yes—probably an under-the-table payoff. Could be he was making sure the captain took good care of us— whatever that means. Bet the Priest wouldn't be happy about it, though."

Andy nodded. "I thought the same thing. Alvaronz seems like a decent enough guy."

"Decent enough for a crook, don't you mean?" observed Dave dryly. "Regardless of his intentions, we have to make our move in the next hour, or it may be too late. I vote we take out the guards when they come back. We can dress in their clothes and lock them in this cabin. Hopefully, no one will be looking for us until they've sailed."

"Okay," agreed Andy. "Then we search around for a smaller boat and follow the shore to a radio or telephone, right?"

"Right," said Dave. "You tear strips from the blanket to tie up the guards. Save the pillow cases to carry any food and supplies we can find. I'll break a couple of the legs off this chair to use as weapons."

Those preparations completed, the boys sat down and leaned against the bulkhead to rest—their homemade billy clubs tucked under folded arms. Fatigue soon overwhelmed them, and in spite of their resolve, both were soon asleep.

As midnight approached, activity reached a frantic pitch. The captain restlessly paced the deck, his impatience showing in fits of rage. Any slackers involved readying the ship for sailing was threatened with a boot or a fist. No one dared to challenge the brutal master of the ship. Every man connected to this illegal venture knew that failure to be at sea before the sun's first light could put them all in jeopardy.

The boys locked in the tiny cabin were forgotten for the moment while holds were loaded and hatches secured. The tall exhaust stacks began to stream sooty, black clouds of smoke as fuel oil fed the boiler fires. The first mate reported that steam would be up within the hour. A tug radioed its arrival would be around the same time, to turn the freighter and escort it out of the channel.

The last skids of food and engine repair parts arrived on a battered truck. Two forklifts scurried up the aft ramp to transfer the cargo to the hold. The loadmaster on the main deck kept up a constant stream of curses and warnings through his bullhorn, as he goaded the dockworkers and sailors to get the ship underway.

As the final forklift load disappeared into the aft hull, the forward gangway was being hoisted ashore. At the same time, the undocking tug was approaching the last curve before reaching the *Star.*

Time was running out and the inability to stay awake was robbing the Carvers of every precious second.

CHAPTER XVII
Jumping Ship

"Captain—tug's comin'," shouted a scruffy seaman from the dockside. He pointed far down the river to a powerful spotlight sweeping slowly from bank to bank. The tug would be alongside in no more than ten minutes.

The freighter's whistle hooted a greeting to the approaching tug, and the captain ducked into the pilot house to grab the mike. "Mate to the bridge. All hands prepare to cast off. Make lively unless you want to meet up with the Federales—we need to be past the point before sunup."

The booming voice startled Dave out of his catnap and it was a few moments before he remembered where he was. Lack of sleep was telling at a time when both boys needed to be most alert.

"Andy. ANDY! Wake up!" urged Dave.

"Wha...what's happening?"

"They're getting ready to cast off, and no one's come to check on us. We've got to get someone's attention and I think I know how! Crouch down against the wall in that corner and start groaning like you have the worst stomach ache in the world. I'll call for help."

Andy sagged to his knees and rested his head against the steel bulkhead at the farthest corner from the door. He began to groan in a convincingly painful manner and rocked from side-to-side.

"Somebody—help. My cousin's sick and needs a doctor. Help me! Please—help!"

A sailor standing near the stern line crossed to the door and peeked through the porthole. "Shut up the racket, kid. We're getting under way."

"Please," begged Dave. "Andy's really sick. I think the meat we got earlier was bad. He needs to go to the head and to get a drink of water. I heard the captain say he needed to talk to us after we sail, so I know he doesn't want anything to happen to Andy."

The sailor knew that the journey was destined to be a short one for their *guests*, but he couldn't take a chance on whether or not the boy was telling the truth. If the captain did want to question them and the kid died, it would probably be his neck. This monster of a captain might even make him join the surviving kid in the shark-infested water.

"All right, stop your cryin' and move back into the corner, and I'll have a look at him." With that, he unlocked the door and pushed inside.

Dave was huddled against the far bulkhead when the sailor bent over his groaning cousin. He grasped the boy by his shaking shoulders and jerked him away from the wall.

Andy made a retching sound and lurched forward, pulling the sailor off balance. Dave sprang forward and brought the chair leg down on the back of the seaman's head. With a low groan, the man slid to the floor and lay quiet.

"You didn't kill him, did you?" asked a white-faced Andy.

Dave felt for a pulse, then shook his head. "He'll be out for a while, but he's okay. Help me get his clothes off and we'll gag and tie him."

"The smell of his clothes is enough to gag me," said Andy. "I hope you're the one who plans to wear them." With that, he knelt beside the man and helped Dave undress him.

"He seems big enough that I can put his jacket and pants over top of my own clothes until we get off the ship. If anyone sees us, I'm just one of the sailors who's been told to bring you to the captain."

"Gotcha. What about him?" Andy asked, pointing to the still figure on the floor. "He might come to and cause a racket that'll bring someone to find him."

"I don't think he'll wake up any too soon, but if he does, the gag will keep him from crying out. Use those strips you tore from the sheets to tie him to the cot, then cover him up with a blanket. Once we're clear of the ship and it sails, they're sure to find him, but there's no way they'll return for us."

"Maybe so, but you can bet they'll radio back to the base. Alvaronz and his boys will be after us in a heartbeat.

Worse still, that Cowboy character may get hold of us." He shuddered at the thought.

Dave finished buttoning up the evil-smelling jacket, then stooped to run his hand along the filthy floor, and smeared the greasy dirt on his face and hands. His disguise was complete.

"Come-on," he said. "I'll step outside and check to see if it's clear. Anyone who sees me will think I'm our sleeping friend here." He pulled open the door and stepped boldly into the floodlit night. Men were hustling in every direction, paying no attention to him.

"Hey—you—yes, you lazy pig, I mean you," shouted a gravely voice.

Dave spun around to discover a huge, red-faced man pointing at him from atop one of the hatches.

"Man that line and stand by."

Dave lowered his voice and his eyes as he replied. "Get somebody else. Cap'n told me to bring this brat to his cabin. He plans to have a lil' bon voyage chat with 'im."

The man grunted and hurried off to draft another to the task of tending the stern line. Dave ran quickly back into the cabin, grabbed Andy by the arm, and dragged him out onto the deck, slamming the door behind him.

"Get fo'ard, kid. The Cap'n wants you to 'ave tea and cookies wif him," he ordered, giving Andy a hard push. Dave winked at a nearby sailor as they passed. The man grinned knowingly.

"Not so rough," hissed Andy as he stumbled over a coil of rope.

Dave whispered back, "We better make it look real or we'll both know what rough is really like. Keep up the act of being frightened."

"It's no act."

"Hey, where you goin' with the kid?" challenged the forklift operator at the aft gangway.

"First mate saw 'im toss somethin' in the bushes just before 'e came aboard. Told me to take 'im down where the jeep stopped and make 'im show me what it was," said Dave in his butchered imitation of a Cockney sailor.

"Oh, yeah?" said the driver. "What makes you think he'll cooperate?"

"Simple. We still got 'is cousin in the cabin. E'll do what E's told or the other kid 'its the river with a hunnert-pounds a chain on 'is legs. Yeah. Sing like a lit'le birdie, 'e will. Say, 'ows 'bout a lift on yer fork?"

"Well, all right. I gotta be getting off this rust bucket, anyway. Make it snappy; they're ready to haul the gangway aboard in about ten minutes, so you don't have all day to nose about."

Dave shoved Andy onto an empty skid that was threaded onto the forks and jumped on next to him. The driver began backing down the gangway. No one took notice of them as they cleared the dock and headed for the spot where the jeep had been parked. The driver and Dave jumped off. Andy was hauled bodily from the skids.

"Kinda dark over here," observed the driver. "I'll turn the fork and use the headlights to make it easier to see."

Dave quickly pulled out the flashlight he'd taken from the old truck. "Never mind. This'll do. Show me where you tossed whatever the mate saw, kid," said Dave threateningly.

"Over there—by that bush," directed Andy, playing the terrified role in a convincing manner. Given Dave's rough treatment and the dangerous situation they found themselves in, it was rather easy to do.

The curious forklift driver accompanied them to the bush. He leaned in, parting the branches to see if he could be the first to spot the mysterious object that the kid was supposed to have flung there. Dave glanced back at the ship. No one was taking notice of them. Silently, he slipped the chair leg from his jacket sleeve. There was a dull thud and the man fell half-way into the bush, an egg-sized lump beginning to rise on the back of his head.

Dave flipped him the rest of the way into the branches, then reached in to feel the man's neck for a pulse. He would live, but like the sailor in the cabin he'd have a headache to remember.

"Quick," said Dave. "Get on the forklift and hang on. We're heading out of here while everybody's concentrating on sailing."

Just as he spoke, the tug maneuvered past the freighter in preparation for swinging *The Black Star*'s bow down river. Activity was at a frantic peak now as the second gangway was taken aboard and the crane was stowed.

The boys scrambled aboard the forklift. Dave was quickly able to figure out the controls, then he shifted into low gear and eased out on the clutch. Seconds later they were rolling down the bumpy trail toward the base.

Behind them, hawsers that held the ship to the land were freed and winched aboard. Cargo doors clanged shut in the side of the hull and the oily smoke doubled in volume as it poured from the twin stacks.

Andy stood on the skids and leaned out far enough to see back around the lift's uprights. Not a soul paid attention to their departure, much to his relief. His heart skipped a beat when he saw a stirring in the bushes and watched in horror as the forklift driver staggered out into the clearing. He waved his arms wildly above his head as he wobbled toward the ship.

On the bridge, the first mate shook his head in disgust and pointed out the man to the captain. "Look at that drunken fool. We're lucky he slept through the loading or he might have caused serious damage."

"Don't worry about it. This is probably the last cargo we haul for those crazy thieves. Wave back at him and let's get underway."

Andy could finally catch his breath as *La Estrella Negra* began moving slowly from the dock, then easing toward the center of the river where the idling tug waited. In short order the tug had swung the freighter's bow around one-hundred-eighty degrees, and the freighter with its cargo of stolen art—and its crew of thieves and murderers—was on the way to Venezuela.

In the small aft cabin, the bound and gagged sailor stirred under the blankets that covered him, and moaned loudly. With the twenty-foot propeller sloshing noisily beneath him no one heard his muffled cries for help.

CHAPTER XVIII
A Change Of Destination

As they neared the base, Dave throttled the forklift down to a crawl. Andy, sitting on the skid, held the flashlight near the ground, only a thin slice of light showing between his fingers. He was the first to spot the faint glow in the distance and quickly switched off his torch.

"Up ahead, Dave. That must be the base. Looks like light coming from the hut that Alvaronz uses for an office. We better go on foot from here."

Dave shut off the engine and slipped to the ground. The jungle was as dark as India ink He had to run his hand along the fork to where Andy waited. "Let me have the flashlight. Hang on to me and I'll feel our way to the edge of the clearing. I won't turn it on unless I really have to."

Andy wrinkled his nose at the smell of the jacket. "Can't you get rid of that thing first? The owner must never have been introduced to a bar of soap in his life."

"Hey, I'm not crazy about it either, but if we're spotted it might be the best chance we have of talking our way out of being captured again. Worked on the ship."

Andy hooked a finger through Dave's belt loop. They felt their way through the blackness, concentrating on the light ahead. Arriving at the clearing, they crouched behind several large packing crates and listened. Nothing moved. The only sound was loud Mexican music spilling from a radio in the hut.

Andy leaned close to Dave's ear. "Shouldn't we head for the North end of the runway and push through to the beach? The Gulf waters didn't seem that far away when we landed."

"At over 200 kilometers per hour, it's farther than you think. If we took only two minutes to fly from the beach to the end of the runway, that would be over six kilometers of jungle between us and the sea. If we made it through all that, we'd have to be lucky enough to find a boat, and even luckier to find civilization within a short distance. We wouldn't even know which way to go once we cleared the surf."

Andy strained to make out his cousin's face in the pale glow from the hut window. "You mean we've gone though all of this, and you don't even think we have a prayer of getting out of here?"

"Would you rather take your chances at sea with that gang of cutthroats? Don't get yourself in a knot. I still have a couple of ideas. Remember how we talked about stowing away on a plane? Cowboy said he had to flush the tanks in the Lear before he could fly out of here. Look over by the hangar. You can just see one of the wing tanks showing through the door. He hasn't left yet."

Without further discussion, the boys began to weave their way around and between machines, boxes, drums, and trees to the back of the hangar. Only a small work light illuminated the interior of the building. No sounds came from inside.

Andy followed Dave as he felt his way along the hangar wall bordering the jungle. They were about to turn the corner by the huge sliding doors when a metallic clang, followed by a stream of curses in English, stopped them. Someone was near the jet.

Dave dropped to all fours. Slowly he began to crawl toward the narrow opening between the doors. Keeping his head low to the ground, he eased forward until he could just make out a section of the sleek aircraft's belly. He saw snakeskin boots standing in a puddle of fuel on the far side of the fuselage. It had to be Cowboy, working at the wing vents.

The clang had been a dropped wrench which still lay nearby. Somewhere out of their sight, a pump hummed. A pulsing hose crossed the floor carrying fresh fuel to the Lear. They were just in time.

Dave slid back into the shadows and explained his plan to Andy. "We'll have to slip aboard while he's coiling the fueling hose. The jet's passenger door is open, and Cowboy seems to be alone. If we can find somewhere to hide on the plane until he gets airborne, we should be able to force him to take us to the airport in New Orleans."

"Who would've thought the Carver Cousins would end up being hijackers?" said Andy. "For that matter, it's hard to believe we've held people at gunpoint and knocked others out with chair legs. What will our moms say?"

"They'd probably say, 'Have some more cookies—and quit playing with those bad guys,' " suggested Dave with a smile. Andy pictured that scene and grinned in return, although Dave didn't notice in the darkness of the Yucatan night.

It was a half hour later before Cowboy finished storing the hose and entering flight information into the onboard computer. He left the jet, and walked through the hangar doors out into the night. Passing within twenty feet of the boys, he strode purposefully toward the office.

"Quick. Now's our only chance," whispered Dave. "Get through the hangar opening as fast as you before anyone sees us silhouetted against the light. Make straight for the plane. We've got to find a place to hide before Cowboy returns."

Breathing heavily with exertion and excitement, the boys scrambled aboard. They crouched in the dark interior, listening for footsteps. The cockpit glowed with dozens of colored lights from various instruments and switches. Electricity was generated by the ground power unit, which was connected to the aircraft in preparation for engine starting.

"How about squeezing into the closet behind the cockpit?" suggested Andy.

"No good. I'm sure he has some luggage. That's the first place he'll go. There are a number of wooden crates strapped in the aisle between the seats in the back. They probably are blocking the door to the restroom. If we can move them forward a foot or two and re-strap them, we can hide in the head until we're in the air."

Moving with stealth and desperation, the boys shifted the crates. One of the lids was loose and Dave lifted up a corner, then carefully shined his flashlight beam inside. Wrapped in straw were small and delicate animal carvings. There was also a pottery doll modeled after an Incan priest.

He took the doll and one of the animals and handed them to Andy to put into his jacket pocket. They strapped down the crates again, and then crowded into the tiny restroom.

Andy had been concerned that Cowboy would notice the extra weight in the tail as soon as he began to trim out for flight. Dave assured him that moving the heavy crates forward should compensate for their combined weight. Besides, it was unlikely that he would land again just to check on the slight imbalance.

Andy's stomach growled loudly in the dark, crowded space. They had eaten very little after the Anaconda sandwich surprise.

"Shhh," warned Dave. "Cowboy could hear that clear up front if he were here."

"Oh, sure. All I have to do is tell my stomach to knock it off, and it will suffer in silence. Wait a minute. I forgot that I brought some real food—meat and cheese from the shed, and a bottle of water."

The boys ravenously devoured every scrap and drank the last drop of bottled water from the supply in the pillow case Andy pulled from his shirt. The hasty snack would give them strength for the ordeal ahead.

The grating of rollers badly in need of oil signaled that Cowboy Ritter was opening the hangar doors. They could hear him talking to another man, but the conversation was too muffled for the boys to understand. Dave's mind was racing. Did this mean there would be more than one crook aboard? If so, their chances were not good at all. He had counted on Ritter being too occupied with flying to put up any resistance. If others were involved, he would have to rethink their strategy.

Fortunately for them, the second man was only there to disconnect the GPU after engine start and to close the hangar when the jet was gone. The clunk of the stairs being raised and the *kerchunk* of the door lock sliding home told them that they were minutes away from lift off.

Outside, the GPU grew louder as the Lear began to draw current into its port starter motor. The whine of the spooling turbine right next to the restroom grew higher in pitch and volume as the igniters lit off the fuel. The powerful jet engine began to turn on its own. The second engine wound up adding its voice to the first. The GPU was disconnected, and the aircraft pivoted toward the hangar opening, bumping lightly over the door tracks.

The boys began to breathe easier as the plane gathered speed, picking its way in the dark to the unlit runway. Cowboy, unaware of his unwelcome passengers, concentrated on the full-time job of piloting the jet. He rolled to a stop at the head of the runway and keyed his radio. "Ready. Give me lights until I clear ground. Then kill them in case someone's watching up there."

Instantly, carefully hooded lights on each side of the runway outlined the path that ended in thick jungle undergrowth. There was no room for mistakes. Cowboy switched on the aircraft's powerful headlights, shoved the throttles to the stops, and released the parking brake.

The roar of the twin jets was deafening to the boys even though they had clamped their hands over their ears. They were plastered against the rear bulkhead as the Lear lunged toward its rotation speed of one-hundred thirty-five knots. Cowboy frowned at the abnormal time it took to get up to speed, unaware that he was carrying an unanticipated additional three hundred pounds in the restroom.

The slim aircraft leapt from the ground with less than five hundred feet of runway to spare. As the wheels retracted, the lights below died, and the jungle swallowed all signs of life in total blackness. They were homeward bound.

Fifteen minutes out over the Gulf of Mexico the radio crackled in the pilot's headset. The unmistakably accented baritone of Señor Alvaronz addressed Cowboy. "I just received an urgent message from *La Estrella Negra*—the boys knocked out a guard and escaped from the ship. I've got everyone searching for them now. They may have headed for the coast, or they may still be on the base."

"Don't tell me about it," retorted Cowboy. "They're your problem now, and when the Priest hears that you've bungled it, you'll have a bigger problem. Adios, Alvaronz." He laughed without humor, switched the radio frequency to that of his destination, and hung his headset on the hook by his seat. Idiots—all of them. He'd be so glad when payoff day comes. He adjusted his seat, checked his instruments, and settled in for the long flight.

Behind him, the restroom door eased carefully open and two darkened shapes emerged into the main cabin, blending in with the bulkiness of the crates in the aisle. Crawling the length of the divans on either side, Dave and Andy began to work their way toward the cockpit.

Cowboy grunted and stared at the artificial horizon instrument. The jet had begun to assume a slight nose-down position. It couldn't be from the fuel burnt during takeoff— the pumps were supposed to keep the tanks trimmed automatically. The instinctive concern for details that comes with being a pilot kicked in. Maybe the crates shifted. It could mean disaster if one of them broke loose. He adjusted the trim, switched on the auto-pilot, and released his seat belt. As he attempted to push himself up, he felt something hard against the back of his head.

"Hello, Mr. Ritter. Thanks for letting us fly 'El Bandito Airlines' again. We enjoyed our little vacation, and now we'd appreciate a lift back home. Now—don't make me use this," said Dave, poking the chair leg firmly against the pilot's neck.

"You kids are totally nuts. You won't do a thing to me 'cause I'm the only one that can fly this jet. Now do yourself a favor and strap into a seat. I don't have any use for you. As far as I'm concerned, you're both still back in the jungle. Be nice, and I'll let you sneak off the plane at the end of the runway when I land."

"Nice try, Cowboy. We both can identify you, and you know it. You have no intention of letting us walk away, and we have no intention of being captured again. The only difference is that now we're armed and you're not. Andy found your gun and holster in the closet, and it fits him nicely."

Cowboy huffed in exasperation. "You're tellin' me that I'm being hijacked with my own gun?"

"No," said Dave, his voice thick with a Southern accent. "Jus' with this lil' old chair leg at the moment." He moved it in front of the pilot's eyes for his inspection. "Of course, Andy's taking over for me, and he prefers your shiny western six-gun to my dull piece of second-hand furniture."

"You boys haven't got a chance of pulling this off," the pilot said. "When we land you'll be outnumbered ten to one by the my guys."

Dave ignored his treat. "I believe I'll make myself at home in the copilot's seat and help you navigate to Stockbridge."

"That's not where we're headed," snapped Cowboy.

"Sure it is," corrected Andy as he cocked the hammer on the six-shooter.

CHAPTER XIX
A Nasty Surprise

Dave settled into the right seat and began leafing through the charts, while Andy folded down the observer seat and held a steady pistol on their unwilling pilot. For twenty minutes not a word was spoken. Then Dave pushed a chart in front of Cowboy's face.

"There's Stockbridge. Reprogram the computer to get us home by the most direct route."

"Tell you what. You're so smart, kid, why don't *you* do the programming?" challenged Cowboy, his arms folded tightly across his chest. "You guys said you wanna learn to fly—here's your chance."

Andy leaned forward and placed the barrel of the pistol against the seat of Cowboy's jeans. "To repeat a recent quote, 'Be nice and I'll let you off the plane at the end of the runway when we land.' On the other hand, be naughty and you'll have to sit crooked the rest of your life, if you get my meaning." He jabbed the pilot's hip with the gun a couple of times for emphasis.

"You mean that? If I take you guys to Stockbridge and park the jet at the far end of the runway, you won't interfere with my leaving?"

"That's right," said Dave. "If you get caught after that, it'll be all your own fault. I know you heard about us turning the guard loose after he led us out of the mine. We're making you the same offer."

Cowboy's jaw worked as he pondered the options of trying to overpower the two boys or going along with them then making his escape. The decision might not be all that difficult since he wanted to get away from that crazy Priest as well. He had some money stashed away, and he still had several crates of stolen art aboard the plane. At any rate, he still had a few hours to think about it. He nodded his agreement.

"Give me the headset," ordered Dave, "and dial up a stateside frequency. We need to send Lieutenant Parker and his men to the church."

Cowboy reached overhead to trip several breakers. The radios blinked out. "Sorry, guys. But no conversation 'til I get clear of the plane. I don't want anyone waiting for me at the airport. I'll restore the radios just before we land and not before. Don't try to figure out which ones are which. You're liable to trip the wrong one and send us diving into the mountains."

Dave shrugged and handed the charts to the pilot, who began entering the new coordinates that would take them home.

Lieutenant Parker sipped gingerly from the scalding cup of coffee that Karen Carver had placed before him, along with a plate of her every-present cookies.

"I'm sorry, Mr. and Mrs. Carver, but the fact is we still haven't found the boys' four-wheelers yet. They had apparently parked them behind an old barn near the hillside church for a while. A small puddle of oil there may have from one of the bikes. Looks like they might have been there at least overnight. Later, they were driven out of the barn. The tracks led down into a shallow creek with a gravel bed. We traced up and down for more than a mile in either direction, but could not find another trace of knobby tracks."

"How about footprints?" asked Karen.

"That's the worrisome part. There were several different types. We surmised from the footprints they made where the bikes were parked, that the basketball shoes belonged to Dave and Andy. There were also heavy work boot tracks and imprints from a pair of cowboy boots. All those came from where a heavy duty van was parked. One tire track had the same half moon cut as the plaster cast we made in your yard.

"We're questioning people along the lower road to learn if anyone saw such a vehicle and could identify it. Of one thing we are certain—the van had recently stopped at the old church. But we haven't learned what the driver and passengers were doing there."

196

Mr. Carver, who had been staring out of the kitchen window toward the mountain, turned to face the detective. "Have you searched inside the church?"

"To be honest, we have looked in through a broken window, but until we get an official search warrant, we cannot legally enter the building. The property is still deeded to the original group that built and owned it. We're processing a warrant to gain access and plan to check it out tomorrow."

Detective Parker stood up and buttoned his coat. "I take responsibility for allowing them to get involved in the art theft case. It may not have anything to do with their disappearance, but I won't rest until they're found. I'll see myself out. Thanks again for the coffee and delicious cookies." With that, he picked up his notebook. Nodding his good-byes, Detective Parker headed for his car and home.

Andy couldn't keep from yawning. It seemed like forever since he'd had a decent night's sleep. Four hours of the monotonous drone of the twin Garrett turbofan engines had produced a lulling effect. Dave was absorbed in studying the instrument panel, pleased that he understood as much about the gauges and displays as he did. He didn't notice his cousin's sleepiness until Andy's head fell against Cowboy's shoulder. Instantly, the pilot reached back and grabbed the barrel of the gun, wresting it away from his groggy captor.

Andy, jolted awake, stared uncomprehendingly at his empty right hand. Cowboy was pointing the revolver at the younger Carver's stomach.

"Well, well. Shoe's on the other foot now, boys. Ol' Tex is back in the saddle. You—get back in the cabin," he said to Andy. "Don't make me shoot your cousin just 'cause you decide to be a hero." He grinned at Dave. "Now—shall we reset our course for our original destination?"

"I don't think so," came the grim answer. "It's still Stockbridge or nowhere!"

Dave flipped off the autopilot and shoved the controls forward. The slim aircraft nosed into a suicide dive, airspeed climbing quickly toward the point-eight Mach maximum operating limit. Above that, the Lear might begin to shake violently, making it almost impossible to control.

"You fool," yelled Cowboy, grabbing the yoke. The gun made it impossible for him to handle the controls with the steady hand needed to recover in time. He made no move to prevent Dave from snatching the weapon from his lap as he struggled with plummeting jet. Perspiration poured from his forehead as he coaxed the Lear into level flight at a safe altitude. Cowboy was breathing heavily by the time he was able to switch back to the autopilot.

"That was crazy. You have no idea how lucky we were to pull out without ripping the wings off this plane. We could've all been killed."

"Better all of us than just the two of us," retorted Dave. "We're going to Stockbridge, and that's that. One more attempt to change our destination and your free walk away is cancelled, understand? We'll leave you cuffed to the yoke and send Lieutenant Parker to pick you up. Last warning. We land in about one hour, and it's almost time to request clearance. If you don't trust me to keep quiet about your involvement, then I'll let you make the call, but play it straight."

Andy had climbed back into the instructor pilot's seat, and Dave surrendered the gun to his cousin. "Stay awake, Andy. We'll be on the ground in less than an hour. Then you can get all the sleep you want. For now, you have to keep an eye on our tricky friend here."

Viewed through the windscreen, the snow-capped mountains marched ever-closer, and the Colorado River wound its snake-like way through the foothills below them. Soon they would be seeing the familiar and welcome sights of Andy's hometown...the library, the City Hall, the airport with its elevated railway, the Carver home and barn, and the old church where this misadventure had begun.

Dave jabbed his finger toward the radio, and Cowboy sullenly restored the breakers. The in-ceiling speakers jumped to life with air traffic reporting in from all around them. As they approached the landing pattern, several commercial and private aircraft could be seen queuing up for their turns to land.

Cowboy dutifully made the call and was instructed by the tower to fall in behind a much larger private jet, a white and red Gulfstream II that was maintaining a holding orbit. According to the flight controller, a departing corporate aircraft had experienced steering problems and was being towed off the runway.

The tower estimated a fifteen minute delay. Dave's nerves were not in any condition to withstand much more in the way of testing, but he knew that remaining calm and in control was vital.

Abruptly, the Lear's fire klaxon rasped out a warning. Cowboy quickly scanned the panel. "We have a fire in the port engine," he said grimly as he punched the fire bottle button and went through shut-down procedures. "Probably still have some contaminants in the fuel."

"What now?" asked Andy, his heart racing.

"We declare an emergency and request immediate landing instructions."

"What about the crippled plane on the runway?" Dave asked.

"If they can't open the runway, we'll have to use one of the small corporate strips in the area."

The boys tightened their seatbelts as Cowboy called in their emergency. The tower cleared the traffic from in front of them and dispatched emergency vehicles to the runway. Dave could see the sudden increase in activity as the ground crew worked to connect the tow-tractor to the disabled plane in their path.

The Lear was sluggish in the crosswind. Cowboy ordered Dave to take over the duties of trimming to compensate for drift. "You know where the gear levers are?"

"Yes," said Dave pointing.

"When I tell you, pull the levers. Let me know when you get all three green lights. We only have one chance at this. I've got my hands full, so you'll also have to help with the flaps. That's the control at your left hand."

Dave nodded, poised and ready to do whatever was needed.

"This is Stockbridge tower. Can you hold altitude for another ten minutes?"

"Negative," said Cowboy. "We've shut down our port engine. We may have contaminated fuel that will take our starboard engine at any moment. We're leaving the pattern and diverting to a private strip."

"Roger. The Corvelle Corporation strip is jet-rated and located ten miles southeast of your present position. Head two-seventy degrees and descend to three-thousand. We'll call the field for clearance and dispatch emergency vehicles to that location."

"Roger, tower. Diverting now."

Cowboy checked his heading and then scanned the instruments.

Dave shielded his eyes against the afternoon sun and searched the southeast quadrant for any sign of a runway.

In the distance, he could see the flashing green and white of a beacon.

"There," he said, pointing. "That must be Corvelle."

"It's no good," grunted the pilot. "I can't hold her. There's a runway straight ahead. It appears long enough. Ready to give me flaps."

The nose of the jet began to slope downward and the buffeting increased as Cowboy eased power back on the remaining turbofan. "Flaps twenty."

"Twenty flaps," answered Dave as he adjusted the controls.

"Gear down."

From the belly of the aircraft came a rumbling sound followed by the drag and whoosh of dropping gear. Three solid clunking noises sounded. Dave declared, "All green."

"Flaps thirty," said Cowboy through clenched teeth. He had to bodily wrestle the jet onto the glide path without the balancing thrust of the second engine. "Full flaps. Brace yourselves—we're going to hit hard!"

The Lear struck forcefully on one main gear and bounded back into the air. Cowboy pulled the yoke tight against his stomach and reduced the throttle setting. The jet settled with a thump on both mains and then drifted down onto the nose wheel. Quickly, the pilot triggered the thrust reverse on the starboard engine and slammed the throttle forward. Dave, at Cowboy's order, helped stand on the brakes while holding full right rudder.

Engine screaming, brakes squealing, tires smoking; the Lear slalomed ever closer to the end of the runway. At the last possible moment, Cowboy slued the aircraft into a left turn and closed the throttle. With a sigh, the turbine began to spool down as the tortured and over-heated brakes squealed the jet to a stop.

They were down—they were in one piece.

Suddenly, Cowboy rammed the throttle forward, steered one-hundred-eighty degrees and headed for the approach end of the runway.

"What are you doing?" demanded Dave, pointing the pistol at the pilot.

"Helping you keep your promise. I'm leaving you guys to explain how you got here while I disappear into the woods. All I ask is a ten-minute head start. It'll take the ground crew that long to catch up to us."

It was almost a mile to the end of the concrete, and another two thousand feet to the forest. The jet ran off the hard surface and bounced across the packed ground. The pilot skidded into a left turn near an old building, and the Lear dipped forward as he brought it to a complete stop. He was at the door and operating the latch before Dave could loosen his seatbelt.

"See ya, boys," he said as the door opened. The steps unfolded to the ground. "Good luck. You're gonna need all you can get." He was gone.

Dave sat dumbfounded. It had all happened so fast. How had he lost control of the situation, and where did this unmarked runway come from.

He turned to his cousin. "We need to get to a phone so the police can take charge of this plane. Make sure we've got the maps and charts that show where we've been."

Andy stuffed the pistol into the map case, stood and folded the IP seat up against the passage wall. Then he followed Dave toward the door on wobbly legs. When his cousin jerked to a stop, Andy collided with Dave's back, and they both tumbled out onto the ground. Andy recovered enough to sit up, and saw the reason for Dave's sudden halt. They were surrounded by a welcoming party made up of several men from the mine, and—*the Priest*!

CHAPTER XX
Race For Life

"Hello, my young friends," said a coldly familiar voice. "How thoughtful of you to help in returning my aircraft, and to visit with me again. I understand you didn't enjoy your little Yucatan vacation. No matter. You're just in time for our retirement party." The improbable leader of the gang of art thieves nodded to one of his men. "Take them to the van."

Dave and Andy stood frozen inside the aircraft cabin in stunned silence.

"You heard the man," came the unmistakable voice of Cowboy. "Welcome back to our little hideaway. While you were occupied with flaps and gear, I switched the radio to a reserved channel and locked the mike in transmit. The guys heard every word we spoke and knew we would land here."

Dave glared at him. "If it hadn't been for that engine fire, the shoe would have been on the other foot."

Ritter laughed. "Actually, there was no emergency. A little sleight of hand and one can create some neat effects. You were concentrating so hard on getting home that it was easy to rattle you with the klaxon test. The rest was just good acting on my part. You might call it a payback for that fake cigarette lighter thing you pulled on us at the church. Now get in the van before the tower discovers where we've set down."

Several men were moving the crates out of the Lear, as another pilot was slipped into the left seat. By the time the van was loaded, both engines on the jet were cranked up, and in minutes the Lear was taxied toward the runway, bound for a safe location.

Within the hour, the van was wending its way through the streets of Stockbridge, although Dave and Andy, sitting on the floor, had no idea where they were being taken. The ride became bumpier as the vehicle left the paved roads and began to claw its way up the dusty trail to Killigan's Gorge.

Cowboy, at the wheel, picked up his cellular phone, punched in number, and mumbled something in a low tone to the answering party. Then he turned to glare down at his captives. "You boys have always wanted to see how we disappeared. Get up and check out what's ahead."

The Carvers pulled themselves up and held onto the seat back. The van was stopped at the edge of the gorge, facing the stone wall across the gap. Andy swallowed at the sight of the empty space in front of them. A few feet more and they would all plunge to their death. Then the bush on the opposite ledge began to move sideways and an opening appeared in the seemingly solid, slate gray face. Like a monstrous mechanical tongue, a steel bridge extended smoothly toward them and came to rest on a lip of stone just below the edge of the chasm.

Cowboy touched his accelerator. The van rolled out onto the phantom bridge and crossed over into the tunnel opening on the other side. They were immediately inside a large cavern where Cowboy swung the van around to face out toward the bridge.

The boys stared in fascination as a man standing at a control panel flipped a series of switches. Smoothly, the bridge retracted into the tunnel Then the opening disappeared as the hidden door with its camouflage bush closed off the light from the setting sun and the outside world. They had escaped death several times, traveled thousands of miles to the Yucatan, hijacked a jet plane, and yet ended up once again in the lair of the criminal leader in cleric robes.

Andy pointed to a spot near the control panel. A quantity of reddish-black fluid was pooled on the rocky floor. Dave nodded as he understood the source of the mysterious stains at several of the theft locations. Footprints crossed through the puddle where men had moved about the chamber.

The hydraulically-operated military bridge had been constructed of surplus parts, but was not maintained as it would have been under an intended government ownership. It was obvious from all of the expense and work that had gone into this elaborate scheme that millions of tax-free dollars were being taken in by the gang.

"Get out," ordered one of the men, pushing the boys through the door of the van.

They were forced to stand as the van was loaded with crates and boxes that had been piled near the bridge. A gray four-wheeler idled next to the freight elevator that had earlier carried them down from the church. The ATV's luggage rack was stacked high with explosives, as was the trailer hitched behind it.

The Carvers surmised that the gang was getting ready to bury everything that would be left in the mine. Given the remarks made by Cowboy, that probably included the men who had been recruited to help with the forgeries and the more labor intensive tasks of crating and shipping the stolen art. They obviously planned eliminate any witnesses. That would, of course, include Dave and Andy.

A driver mounted the ATV and moved carefully forward into the elevator, which then closed and slowly sank from sight. A second four-wheeler and trailer emerged from a side tunnel and pulled to a stop next to a pile of satchel charges. The driver dismounted, carefully laid several charges on the trailer, and then strode over to the elevator to press the return button. The destruction from the explosives would guarantee that any remaining evidence would be buried beyond reach.

Andy prodded Dave with his elbow and nodded toward the idling vehicle. Dave blinked in understanding and stole a quick glance around the large underground room. Everyone seemed to be concentrating on the job of loading the van or on listening to the Priest give final orders for closing down the operation.

"Now!" exclaimed Andy in a hoarse whisper, and the boys broke into a run for their lives to the ATV. Before the men could understand what was happening, the younger Carver vaulted into the seat, while Dave flattened himself on the trailer and clung to the edge. With a ringing whine, the engine revved up, then settled into a powerful growl as Andy kicked lower gear and popped the clutch. He spun in a half circle and headed back into the tunnel.

Bullets cracked into the wall and roof. The boys could hear Cowboy screaming for his men to stop firing. One hit in a satchel charge could have set off the whole pile, killing everyone, the cutthroat gang included. Several hundred feet farther along the tunnel, Andy idled down and switched off the engine. The darkness was complete when the headlights died.

"Think they'll be coming after us?" he asked his older cousin.

"I doubt it. We can't go back. They'll probably set a charge in the tunnel mouth to seal it before they leave. We'll have to go on, and hope there's a way out."

"I'm sure this bike came out of this same tunnel so the driver must have come from somewhere below," reasoned Andy. He started the engine and the ATV crept forward pushing its headlight beams into the bends and creases of the passageway.

The tunnel curved gradually to the right and sloped downward out of sight. Knobby tire tracks in the dust indicated a number of trips up and down the trail. Every hundred yards or so, Andy would shut down so they could listen. Nothing moved. They were alone far beneath the surface—facing death and burial in a matter of minutes.

"Shhh!" urged Dave, although Andy was making no noise unless you counted his heavy breathing. Somewhere ahead in the darkness was the sound of running water. "Ease ahead and let's see where that noise is coming from."

Again, the engine cranked to life. They crept forward until they came to a straight stretch that ended at a blank wall. A steady flow of water gushed from one wall, crossed diagonally in front of them and disappeared into a hole near the opposite side. They splashed through the foot-deep stream and neared the barrier at the end. Andy spotted an opening to the right and slued the four-wheeler into it. A dozen feet ahead they discovered a heavy plank door sealed with a padlock—a satchel charge dangled from the handle.

A faint glow from the numerals on its timer told the boys that there would be no one bothering to come down after them. The Priest had planned to blow the roof this tunnel down, trapping the men on the other side of the door. Every exit must have a similar charge set to explode at the same time. Unless Dave and Andy could think of something fast—they were dead!

Dave leapt from the trailer and sprinted to the door. The numbers read nineteen minutes and were rapidly counting down. There was no room to turn around, no time to go back, and even if they could—there was still the gang waiting.

Andy crowded up beside him. On impulse, the younger cousin grabbed the charge from the door and began running.

Dave was horrified. "What are you doing?" he screamed. "That thing is about to go off!" All he could hear was the scuffling of his cousin's feet off in the darkness. Then came a splash. Then came silence.

"It's okay," Andy's voice said from the blackness. "I dumped the satchel down the hole where the stream emptied. If the water doesn't kill the timer, at least it should be carried all the way down to the river before it explodes."

"Whew! Great job," breathed Dave as Andy moved back into the headlights. "Now we've got to get this door open. You have anything on you to take the screws out of these hinges?"

"No way. Even if I did, they're so old I doubt if we could move them. Maybe we could find rope or cable to hook to the lock and yank it free with the four-wheeler."

They searched the area around the door and discovered a ten-foot length of the quarter-inch threaded rod used by the gang to reinforce the old roof-shoring timbers. Working quickly, and mindful of charges scattered throughout the mine and about to explode, they looped the rod through the padlock hasp and twisted its end around itself. The other end was formed into a similar hook and fastened through a tow eye on the front of the ATV.

Andy eased forward until the four-wheeler was less than a yard from the door. The rod was bowed into a slack curve. He dropped into reverse, raced the engine, and released the clutch. The vehicle lurched backwards and ripped the lock and hasp from the old timbers.

The door was free. Dave jerked it open, revealing a continuation of the tunnel with a faint light in the distance. Frantically, he removed the rod from the vehicle and jumped back on the trailer, hugging the satchels to keep them from falling off. They might be needed later, he reasoned.

A hundred yards farther on, the four-wheeler burst into the huge lighted chamber that the boys recognized as the one they had been brought to when first captured. Dave pointed to the stairs leading to the office, and Andy opened the throttle to take them through the midst of the startled men working there. Before they could be stopped, they were off the ATV and up the stairs. Dave stood at the top with the satchel charge held high above his head. Andy keyed the intercom mike that had been clipped to the office wall.

"Everybody, stay right where you are. I'm sure most of you recognize the type of explosive charge my cousin is holding. It can bring this whole cave down on all of us. If you want to stay alive, you better listen to me."

Shouts of outrage rose from the floor of the cavern below them, but no one attempted to storm the stairway.

"The Priest and his partners are running out on you. They've set these charges at every exit and plan to bring the place down on your heads. If any of you had suspicions that they would not be splitting the money with you at the end, you were right. We escaped from them at the bridge, but they had already fixed the door we came through with explosives. If there's any other way out of here, you better take it right now."

Several of the men edged toward the elevator. When others noticed them, more began moving quickly in the same direction. One man pressed frantically on the button, but there was no response from the silent machinery. With the realization that the priest must have ordered the circuit disconnected, Dave's story rang true to the desperate men.

"See if the phone in there is still hooked up," urged Dave, holding the satchel where all could see.

Andy grabbed for the handset and held it to his ear. "Dead as a doornail. They've cut us off, but good. We're trapped with all of them down there."

"Maybe not," said Dave thoughtfully as he studied the timer on the bomb. "About ten minutes have passed since you dumped the charge down that hole on the other side of the door. That hopefully means there's about nine minutes left before all the charges go off. If we can get back to the old ladder in that passage, we might be able to get down to the river and escape by grabbing a boat or by swimming out."

"We'll never get past those men down there."

"We will if they're afraid of this satchel," replied Dave. "If I can figure how to set it to go off in a minute or two, we might be able to get into the passage and use the explosion to close off the opening behind us. It's risky, but I don't know any other answer."

"That means all these guys will be left in here to die," shuddered his cousin.

"I don't think so. The Priest couldn't have placed enough charges to bring down the whole cave. I think he figured on sealing them in here, knowing that by the time they could be dug out, no one would still be alive. If we can escape, we might be able to help the authorities find a way to get in here in time to save everyone."

"I'm ready when you are," said Andy.

"Good. The timer is simple and I see how it works. I'm setting it for two minutes…Okay, it's set and running—Let's go."

Dave and Andy scrambled down the stairs two at a time. The men by the elevator spotted them and began running towards them.

"Grab the kids," someone yelled. "They must know how to get out of here."

"Yeah," shouted another. "They're headed back the same way. Stop them!"

The cousins reached the passageway that led down to the art vault and sprinted toward the side tunnel leading to the escape ladder. Reaching the junction, Dave stopped and held the satchel up for the pursuers to see.

"This goes off in less than a minute. Get back or the tunnel comes down on your head."

"We ain't fallin' for that line. You'd blow yourself up, too," said one of the men.

"Take your chance, then. Here's your bomb." Dave threw the satchel toward the man. In total chaos, the mob broke ranks and ran—pushing, shouting, and swearing. As the gang members cleared the mouth of the main tunnel, and as the Carvers ducked into the side passage, the satchel charge exploded with a tremendous roar and the pressure wave slammed the boys against the wall.

Andy groaned as his head hit the rocky surface, and he slumped to the floor. It was pitch black. The only light had been from the cavern, which was now closed off by the collapsed roof. Dave felt for his cousin, and found him lying curled up.

"Andy—talk to me. Are you okay? Comeon. Say something."

"Okay, okay. I'll say something. Quit shaking me, or I'll throw up all over you. I hit my head on the wall, and the stars I'm seeing are the only light we've got left to find our way out of here."

Dave laughed in spite of the desperate situation, but quickly returned to the reality of the moment. "I don't know what will happen when the charges all go off, but we have only a few minutes to find the ladder and get down to the river."

"We don't have a flashlight this time. How will we manage in total darkness?"

"By memory. It was only a few dozen yards ahead as I remember. We'll have to crawl and feel our way, but hurry."

Foot by painful foot, they crept forward until Dave's arm reached empty space.

"We're here. Stay put 'til I find the ladder."

He stretched out his arm and swung it back and forth until his knuckles clunked against the familiar rusty metal. "Got it. I'll get on the ladder first, and you follow about ten rungs behind. Remember that some of them are missing and the whole thing is likely to be even more wobbly than on our first trip down."

If their first descent on the ancient steps was scary, this one in total darkness was a thousand times worse. In spite of Dave's warning about missing rungs, they both nearly lost their footing several times when they encountered the gaps. The side rails flexed and the anchor bolts creaked as the ladder threatened to pull loose and plunge them to a horrifying death on the rocks below.

"We must be getting close to the bottom," said Andy without much conviction.

"I don't know—there's no way to tell. I don't even have anything to toss down there. Keep going. The whole thing could collapse when those satchels begin going off."

Suddenly, Dave's left ankle plunged into icy water, and he gasped with the shock. The river had risen from the melting snows and had covered the bottom rungs of the ladder. He dropped with a splash and touched bottom, leaving only his shoulders and face above the surface.

"I'm in the water," he said, his teeth chattering. Let go when you reach the bottom rung. Hurry! We need to see if they've left any boats."

Andy splashed down in the dark, grabbed the back of Dave's jacket, and followed blindly as they waded through the freezing water toward the dock. As they rounded the curve, they could see light, although it was much dimmer than the last time.

"Keep quiet. There still might be some of the men there," warned Dave as he hugged the side of the channel and slowly moved to the cave entrance. He peered around the corner of the tunnel and saw that the dock was deserted except for one remaining boat that was tied up and listing drunkenly to one side.

Andy moved up beside him. "Looks like the only one left has a hole in it."

"We might be able to paddle it out. If not, we'll have to swim for it." Both boys' teeth were chattering from the cold water. They wouldn't last long if they didn't get out of this freezing river. Dave began stroking for the boat, and Andy dog-paddled after him. Dave rounded the stern, climbed the boarding ladder, and peered over the transom. Andy saw the startled look on his cousin's face just before Dave lost his grip and fell back into the water.

Dave's eyes reflected his confusion when he surfaced in front of Andy.

"There's someone lying on the bench seat in the boat," he whispered.

"Is he dead?"

"He wasn't moving then, and he doesn't seem to be now."

Andy swam to the ladder and pulled himself up for a look. "Dave—it's Cowboy—he's unconscious!" Throwing caution to the wind, he scrambled over the side and landed in a foot of water. He was followed quickly by Dave.

They knelt by the man, and Dave felt for a pulse. "He's alive, but not by much."

"Ugh! Look at his leg," exclaimed Andy, wrinkling his nose at the smell and nodding to the rip in the side of Cowboy's jeans. They saw that the pilot's thigh was badly swollen, and that a festering sore oozed from a nasty infection. Now they knew why Cowboy had been limping, but not that the cause had been the puncture from the old chair spring at the church. Even if they could get him to the hospital, he might lose his leg.

Dave jumped to the controls, and seconds later, the engine coughed, sputtered, and caught. There was water in the engine compartment, and the four-banger sounded very rough.

"Cast off and find something you can use to bail with while I get us out of here."

He flipped on the spotlight and eased away from the dock. With nearly a half ton of river aboard, this would not be a speedy retreat, but it was better than swimming.

218

Studying the dash controls Dave found the sump pump switch and heard the gratifying hum as it came to life, spewing a two-inch stream of water from the outlet. He edged the throttle forward another notch.

Andy had ripped away the rest of Cowboy's pant leg and was rummaging through the compartments in the boat for something to drain the ugly wound. He found an old fish scaling knife and a water-proof case with two matches inside. Wiping the knife dry on his shirt tail, he lit both matches and passed the blade back and forth through the flame until his fingertips began to feel the heat.

Returning to Cowboy, he carefully made an incision along the side of the wound. A smelly stream of pale green fluid gushed from the cut, and Andy scraped it away with the blade. He pressed the side of the knife against the leg to force more of the pus out of the opening. Ripping his own shirt into strips, he tied off Cowboy's leg above the infection to prevent the spread of gangrene, and then moved forward to stand next to Dave.

Andy tapped his cousin's shoulder and pointed ahead. "There's the gate made out of brush. I'll see if I can find the switch between those rocks and trigger it with the paddle." He swung the spot light on the rocks and leaned over the side, shoving the paddle blade into the water.

KABOOM! A loud explosion sounded somewhere above and behind them. *KABOOM—KABOOM!* One after another, charges exploded, sealing the exits and trapping men in the main chamber. The boat rocked as a bomb exploded beneath the elevator at the dock.

Just as Andy's paddle connected with the switch A wave rushed toward them. At the same time the gate began to swing open, the back of the boat was lifted on the crest of the wave. They were hurled through the narrow opening and out into the river, under a glorious evening sky filled with bright, clear stars. Behind them several more explosions sounded deep in the cave. Ahead of them lay freedom and safety.

They passed near to the old timbers of the long-fallen bridge and then stared up to the place where the phantom bridge had appeared and disappeared throughout this long week. The boat was getting lighter as the pump continued to empty the water from the bilges. Dave could feel their speed pick up as the water level went down.

Andy crouched next to Cowboy and felt the man's forehead. "He's burning up. I don't know how long he can last with this fever. The gang must have decided he was too much of a risk with that bad leg and left him to die when the bomb went off at the dock."

The loudest explosion of all sounded above and behind them. The boys turned and stared upwards through the darkness within the walls of Killigan's Gorge. They witnessed a fiery eruption of flame and smoke belching from the tunnel they had entered earlier inside the van. Chunks of rock shot from the opening, and then, like the emerging of a giant moray eel, the great bridge squeezed out of the tunnel, tilted slowly, and with a screeching moan of twisting metal, plunged eighty feet into the river below.

Dave throttled back to idle and stared in fascination. "I remember seeing something like that in a movie once. Only instead of a bridge, it was about huge German guns."

Andy's reply was hushed. 'Guns of the Navahos,' I think."

Cowboy stirred and groaned. "Idiot kids. It was 'Guns of *Navarone.*' Where the blazes am I? How did you guys get here? What's happening?"

Dave eased the boat into forward gear and moved down stream again.

"You don't have the right to demand any answers," said Andy, "but we pulled your sorry skin out of the mine as a trainload of bombs started going off. We guessed that your buddies left you to die. How's that for loyalty?"

"It's the breaks," said Cowboy. "I tried to keep anyone from knowing how bad it was until we got away from here, but it got to the point that I couldn't hide the pain and swelling. They had to leave me. If the situation were reversed I'd do the same thing. But who was it that bandaged up my leg?"

"I did. I had to make a cut and drain your wound. You're lucky most honest people don't think the same way as you thieves and murderers do. Nevertheless, you could lose the leg if we don't get you to a doctor soon."

Andy patted down Cowboy's pockets. "Do you have your cell phone?"

"Don't be so stupid, kid. Think the priest would leave one with me to call 911 from the cave?"

Andy ignored the insult. "How long 'til we get to the beach, Dave?"

"We'll be there in a few minutes," came the reply. "I'll have to hoof it to the nearest phone when we land."

That wasn't the case, however, for when they rounded the next curve, the beach was suddenly flooded with the headlights of a half-dozen police cars. A bull-horn warned the boat occupants to show their hands and to head straight for the shore. Dave and Andy were more than happy to comply with those orders.

Several policemen grabbed for the bow rope flung by the younger cousin, and they pulled the prow up on the sand. Dave gave one last burst of the throttle to firmly beach the boat and then switched off the engine. Lined up on either side of them were the rest of the boats from the mine.

"Is that you, Andy Carver?" came a familiar voice.

"Lieutenant Parker. Are we ever glad to run into you. How did you know we'd be here?" said Dave.

"My men were in position up there on the edge of the gorge when they spotted your boat coming out of the tunnel. They radioed me and we prepared a welcome party for whoever was on board. We've arrested at least a dozen men in boats and several in a van full of stolen art work. I guess we got all of them."

"No," declared Andy. "There's a whole bunch more that were trapped down in the old mine by the leader of this gang and his cronies. They planned to bury them alive to leave no witnesses. We have one of the crooks here in our boat. He's been injured and has a serious infection. Do you have any medics with you?"

"Yes. There's an emergency truck with medics up on the road. You men help get the prisoner out of the boat."

While the stricken Cowboy was on his way to the hospital, Andy was drawing a diagram in the sand to show the inspector the layout of the mine.

Dave dropped to his knees and sketched another view. It was a cross section showing the old church with the elevator shaft. "I doubt if you can get the damaged elevator running again, but if you can lower some men down the shaft, you might be able to make your way into the main cavern to rescue any survivors."

The detective quickly gave instructions to the officers surrounding him and turned back to the Carvers. "So, you boys have been held prisoner in the old mine for the last couple of days."

"There's a little more to it than that," Andy declared. Between the two, the incredible story spilled out. At the end, Andy reached into his jacket pocket and verified their account by surrendering the two pieces of statuary taken from the plane. Lieutenant Parker scribbled notes as fast as he could write. Finally, he held up his hand for silence.

"You boys need to get home. Your parents have been worried sick about you. We can finish this briefing in the morning. And don't be too anxious about the men in the cave. Your information has given us several ways to work on getting them out."

CHAPTER XXI
All the Answers—*Almost*

"Dave, I called your mom and dad and they will be here on the earliest flight tomorrow morning. It's so hard to believe that all of this could have happened in such a short time," said a relieved Mrs. Carver. "We've had everybody from the FBI to the Governor involved in finding you."

"What?" exclaimed Dave. "How did you manage that kind of cooperation?"

"The Governor is a close friend of mine," answered Martin Carver. "As a matter of fact, we attended college together. Even more important was the report from the ATF agents who spotted the *S.O.S.* signal from the plane. They suspected that the Lear's flight originated from this area, and your sketch of the jet and your account of what you learned about the gang were wired to all of the surrounding police departments.

"My complaint about the jet that nearly ran into you had been filed earlier with the police, and the authorities were asked to be on the lookout for it. A local inspector got both reports across his desk. It began to add up with other clues."

"How did Detective Parker know to be at the gorge?" asked Andy.

"Another part of the puzzle," offered Mrs. Carver. "They reviewed your report of the disappearing headlights and sent a car to search the area by daylight. They found your ATV tracks and traced them to the edge of the gorge and then up to the old church. They knew that someone had been staying there for a while, but didn't realize that there was an elevator hidden behind the organ pipes in the choir loft."

"So they staked out the old church and the gorge and waited?" suggested Dave.

"Right," said Uncle Martin. "The police spotted the truck when it took you across the bridge, even though they had no idea you were inside. They were planning to rush the mine when the bridge was deployed the next time.

As it turned out, the crooks came to them as one nice package in the van, but before the police could charge across the bridge, someone inside retracted it, and possibly used the elevator to get to the dock. After disabling the elevator, they attempted to escape in the boats and sailed right into their little beach trap."

The doorbell rang, surprising the Carvers, given the lateness of the hour.

Martin opened the door to discover two people dressed in white uniforms, one standing behind a cart piled with containers.

"Mr. Martin Carver?"

"Yes?"

"We're from Blue Mountain Catering. We received a call from the Governor's office to bring you folks a late meal. Said you would probably have a couple of very hungry young men here."

"Wow! You can say that again," said Andy with great enthusiasm.

Everyone laughed as the cart wheeled through the door, and soon the dining room table was covered with an abundance of appetizing courses. The tantalizing odors brought appreciative rumbles from the stomachs of both Carvers.

"Hope you like pot roast, ribs, and fried chicken," said the caterer. "We weren't sure what you liked so we brought a variety. You can freeze what you can't eat and have it later."

"It smells great," said Andy, "and it's bound to beat snake steak."

The caterer had a puzzled look as he and his partner returned to their truck.

"Don't even tell me what that means," said Karen Carver, although she knew she would hear every detail of the story in the near future.

The next morning, a patrol car picked up the cousins and escorted them to the police station where they identified most of the men in the lineup. One face was conspicuously absent—where was the Priest?

"Don't know who you're talking about," said Inspector Parker. "These are the only men we arrested, aside from the one you call Cowboy, and the ones trapped in the mine. Incidentally, the elevator shaft was destroyed, but we've broken through the top of the main chamber. All of the men have survived the explosions. As soon as we enlarge the opening, we'll first remove the injured, and then supply food and water to the rest while they await rescue.

"My men also found your four-wheelers hidden in a stand of trees downstream. I have an idea that the men who left them there had no intention of ditching them in the stream. They undoubtedly planned to retrieve them for their own use later. So much for obeying orders. Now, tell me more about this Priest fellow."

That's exactly what the Carvers did over the next two hours of debriefing. Thanks to the disks Andy recorded at the Yucatan hideout, the database of the gang's customers was sent by modem to Interpol, and *The Black Star* was boarded off the coast of Honduras. Mexican police raided the airbase, and the Colorado State Patrol rounded up more of the gang at the airstrip near Stockbridge.

Two days later, the last of the survivors were brought out of the mine, treated for injuries, and charged with being accessories to grand theft. The recovered plunder was displayed at the local armory. To the great delight of the Carvers, their own stolen artwork had not been shipped out and was soon restored to Martin's office and the family home. The wall that had displayed their now destroyed bas-relief, however, would have to remain bare.

The phone rang in the Carver living room, and Martin answered it. After hanging up, he turned to the boys. "Inspector Parker says the gang member called Cowboy wants to see you. Parker said he would send a police car for you."

"I don't know if I ever want to see him again," responded Andy, eyes flashing with anger.

"Maybe we can find out where the Priest has gone?" suggested his cousin.

"Okay. You're right. I'll call the inspector and tell him we'll be ready. I know it sounds stupid, but do you think we ought to take him some kind of gift? He *is* in the hospital, you know."

"Why not?" said Dave. "He's got plenty facing him after he's well. Besides, he could have treated us worse that he did. Who knows? He might tell us about the plane that he mentioned building. We could get ideas for our own."

"You've convinced me. I'll take my notebook computer and show him my wing lift calculating program."

"Go easy," warned Mr. Carver. "The man is a career criminal. You don't dare forget that for a moment."

The cousins nodded and raced upstairs to gather up the computer and a roll of aircraft construction plans that they wanted to show to Cowboy.

"Hi, guys," greeted a pale-faced Cowboy who sat propped up in his bed in the private ward. The policeman guard took a seat nearby. "What's the matter, cop. You afraid I'll run away?" Cowboy said with a chuckle as he pointed to the sheet that flattened below his knee.

Andy's shock showed on his face. "I'm really sorry you lost your leg. No one deserves a bad break like that."

"Hey, sometimes you win, and sometimes you lose. I asked you guys here to thank you for saving the rest of me. The doc says I would've died from gangrene if you hadn't given me first aid treatment. 'Course, if you hadn't come along, I'd have died from the bombs. Guess I owe you kids a double dose of thanks." He reached out and shook hands with each of them, while the guard kept a wary eye on all three.

"We brought you a couple of things to help cheer you up," said Andy, his eyes watering. "I know it seems weird to give gifts to someone who kept us prisoner, but we feel that you could have killed us back there in the jungle and no one would have been the wiser. You didn't, and that was...uh...nice of you."

Cowboy and Dave burst out laughing at Andy's awkward speech. Instead of getting angry, Andy joined in, and so did the guard. When things got back to normal, Dave handed his carry-all bag to the guard for inspection, and then removed a small model of a Lear Jet from it. He offered it to Cowboy, who expressed surprise at how much the paint job resembled that of the plane he flew.

"I painted it so I'd never forget what the jet that almost ran into my airliner looked like," explained Dave.

"I heard that one of our idiot pilots almost took out a commercial jet and half the mountainside. You were in that plane, huh? Must have been an ugly trip."

"Not one I'd care to take again," agreed Dave.

"Don't know if you have access to a computer where you're going," said Andy, "but I brought you a copy of a program I wrote to calculate wing lift on the aircraft we want to build."

He booted up the notebook and demonstrated the software to his appreciative audience. For the next ten minutes, their former captor described his own experiences as the builder of several single and two-seater aircraft. Then Dave unrolled their construction plans. Cowboy pointed out and corrected several errors.

"There's one thing we'd like to ask you," said Dave, noting that visitation hours were over. "Who is this Priest, and why wasn't he captured with the rest?"

Cowboy seemed surprised by the news that his leader wasn't in custody, but was now willing to tell what he knew of the man.

"Story has it that he served in the priesthood at one time—big church in Canada. They say he liked being a cleric, but also liked the finer things in life—cars, good food, and even artwork. He began replacing his church's valuable art collection with forgeries created by a church member who had revealed his sinful talents during confession. I don't know if he threatened to turn in the forger or only agreed to pay him, but over the years he sold all of the most valuable pieces of art through a fencing network.

"Either the forger squealed or else the quality of the forgeries gave him away. Anyhow, the Priest split, changed his name, and pulled the scam on several more churches before they circulated his picture. He had to come up with a different plan. Visiting in South America, he ran across a fence with international connections, and they worked out the details for this art theft ring. He recruited me in prison, and piloted for him for several years.

"The Priest liked me, and I moved up the ladder as one of his trusted lieutenants. Oh, I also had been in the army, and was able to help get a hold of and to assemble the military bridge we used. Someday, I might tell you what it took to smuggle all those parts into the mine."

The guard checked the time and stood up. "Time to go. The car will be waiting for you boys out front, and Mr. Ritter has an appointment with his doctor. The inspector might let you visit again later."

"One more thing," interrupted Cowboy. He scribbled on the back of a card taken from a vase of flowers on the night stand. "Here's the name and address of my uncle. I've called him and he'll be expecting you. Seein' as how I'll not be going home for a while, and may never get to fly again, there's something I want you to have. In my garage is a brand-new Lycoming one-hundred-eighty horsepower engine that I planned to install in my next home-built. It's plenty big enough to power your two-seater. I want you kids to have it. I'll feel better knowing it's in the hands of guys that will appreciate it and treat it right. Good luck— I...I really mean it."

Dave and Andy were too overwhelmed to do more than mumble their thanks and duck out of the room. Life could be wonderfully strange, but also strangely wonderful.

The next morning, the boys collected the Lycoming from Cowboy's uncle, and it now gleamed proudly on the engine stand in the Carver barn. Their dream came closer by the day.

A substantial reward had been offered by a number of communities for the capture of the art thieves and the return of stolen paintings and other items. After picking up Dave's parents at the airport, Andy's dad dropped off John and Katie's luggage at the house, then the six Carvers made their way to the city hall. When the checks were presented to the Carvers in a televised ceremony, Dave and Andy had a gift of their own for the mayor of Stockbridge.

Andy was invited to step to the microphone. "Mr. Mayor, we appreciate the rewards given to us and will use part of the money for Dave's and my education and to help us realize a few of our dreams. We would also like to present you with our own check as our way of returning a part of the reward money for use by the Miller Galleries.

"Its collection of art has made Stockbridge one of the great cities in a great state. We like to think that it may inspire others to give donations for the replacement of lost artwork and for a new security system." A wild round of applause greeted Andy's speech, and both his and Dave's parents beamed with pride at the generosity of their sons.

Inspector Parker met them as they were leaving the hall and spoke to Dave. "As you've now learned, Dave, Stockbridge has lots of valuable stuff to steal."

Dave blushed at the reference to his earlier remark, and Andy enjoyed the moment.

Parker smiled, then continued. "We found the Priest's robe and collar floating in the river. They were covered with blood. We figure that he was caught in the explosion and blown from the tunnel when the bridge was bombed. We haven't recovered a body and may never find it. The whitewater rapids are not too far south of the Gorge. His body could be halfway to the Gulf by now."

"What if it is a trick?" asked Dave. "He could have shot one of the men, dipped his robe in the blood, and flung it on the bridge before the charge went off. I'm sure he had ways out of there that no one else knew about. We did."

The inspector grinned ruefully. "The case won't be officially closed until unless we find a body, or get word that a church has discovered that one of their ancient religious statues smells suspiciously like fresh modeling clay. Until then there's not a much more we can do.

234

"Unfortunately, we may never know the whole truth about the Priest and his forgery ring. Anyhow, I wanted to thank you, Dave, and you, Andy, for your help. You young men acted like true professionals. Good luck with your college and your airplane." With that, he walked out of the building and was gone.

Lights-out time at the Carvers and the two cousins talked quietly as they lay in their beds. They reviewed the incredible events of the past days, and spoke of the future, specifically of soaring through the sky in their own home-built airplane.

"You know, Dave, there's still one thing that bothers me."

"Yeah? What's that," said his cousin as he fluffed his pillow and yawned.

"Well," said Andy thoughtfully, "I think I've acquired a taste for anaconda sandwiches."

Further comment was snuffed when his face became the target of a pillow skillfully launched from the dark side of the room.

The End